FRIDAY

July 18, 2025

WRONGS & RIGHT

A Maximo Morgan Mystery

JULY

WILLIAM LEROY

All rights reserved. Published by Mossik Press.

mossikpress@mail.com

Library of Congress Cataloguing-in-Publication Data

LeRoy, William [7.29.2025]

Wrongs & Right / Dead Man's Hand
by William LeRoy.

p. cm
ISBN 979-8-9992429-1-4

1. Humor—Fiction.
2. Oklahoma, United States—Fiction.
3. Mystery—Fiction.
4. Noir—Fiction.
I. Title

10 9 8 7 6 5 4 3 2 1

Manufactured in the United States of America
First Edition

WRONGS & RIGHT

JULY

WILLIAM LEROY

CHAPTER ONE

♫*Midnight, one more night without sleeping/ Watching 'til the morning comes creeping...* ♫

Max sat at the bar of an edge-of-town roadhouse called the Second Circle Club, nursing a mug of root beer while eyeing a door at the rear of the barroom and wondering:

♫*Green door, what's that secret you're keeping?* ♫

Above a bright red dot painted on the door — green as a patch of four-leafed clover — a gold-lettered sign said: MEMBERS ONLY.

♫*Wish they'd let me in/ So I could find out what's behind the green door...* ♫

In answer to him asking, a bartender spilled that to become a member of the exclusive inner sub-club a guy had to be a sporting man, and know someone.

"So happens that Yours Truly is tight with a dude named Abe Lincoln," said Max, sliding a light green gratuity across the bar.

"Honest Abes would be out of place behind the green door," said the barkeep, scooping up the five-spot. "But thanks for the tip."

♫*Door slammed, hospitality's thin there/ Wonder just what's going on in there...* ♫

With wallet still in hand, deciding whether to up the ante with a couple of Washingtons...

"Hey, big spender," said a buxom blonde, bulging out of a low-cut red dress and sidling up to his stool. "What's a cat like you doin' out after dark and all by your lonesome?"

He wasn't lonesome, Max explained. His mom, with whom

he had lived since birth, was playing cards with members of her Canasta club, and…

"Aw, that's cold," said the dame, perching herself on the adjacent stool, then batting her baby blues. "Left you without a babysitter."

He didn't mind. He was working a lay, he said, before, uh oh, realizing he might have tipped his hand. If the bim knew Yours Truly was not only a Notary Public, but also a private dick…

"Well, I usually enjoy a glass of bubbly first, but okay. My name's Francesca and I'm a friend of Benjamin."

Yeah, being a chick magnet was an occupational hazard of hardboiled private dicking, and a common complication in undercover investigations of dirty deeds likely afoot.

♪ *Someone laughed out loud behind the green door/ All I want to do is join the happy crowd behind…* ♪

"By the way," he said, "what's with the red dot painted on that green door to a Members Only room?"

"Stands for The Apple," said the skirt. "You know, the forbidden fruit that whets an appetite for 'Original Sin', tee hee."

Original Sin? That was what a bygone Sunday school teacher had pegged as curiosity. In other words, the blonde had made him and…

"Speaking of lust, are you here to 'work' a lay or to get off by just talking about it?"

Max got off the stool, claimed he had to see a man about a dog, and beat feet toward another door at the rear of the barroom signed GENTS. Yeah, according to the Bible, "Original Sin" led to death of curious cats, but…

♪ *Green door, what's that secret you're keeping?* ♪

MONDAY

July 21, 2025

CHAPTER TWO

Okmulgee County District Attorney Hamilton "Ham" Burger paced the floor of his county courthouse office, venting spleen about idiotic idiosyncrasies of the so-called justice system.

Damnit, for last year's successful prosecution of a trans transient, caught passing through the county on a bus from the Mexican border, he had been praised on Fox News by Mark Levin of *Life, Liberty & Levin*. This year he had already cracked down on rampant teenager shoplifting of candy, gum and sundries at convenience stores. With statewide status as a winner in the MAGA fight for restoration of traditional values, next year he would be a leading candidate for Governor. In the meantime, however...

"The law is an ass!" Ham declared, referring to a courtroom setback within the past hour that had made him look like a loser. Specifically, on a technicality—application of the so-called Exclusionary Rule related to constitutional law—old Judge Dwight had thwarted his RICO—Racketeer Influenced and Corrupt Organization—prosecution of the owner/ operator of a veritable den of iniquity on the outskirts of the nearby town of Henryetta.

Though perhaps not literally the Devil incarnate—as some described the man behind the curtain at the Second Circle Club—Durwood "Durndest" Durante, if not actually Satan, was served by Devil's advocates that manipulated contrived legal abstractions and simple words to suit Old Scratch's purposes. By creating confusion about what, say, the meaning of the word "'is' is"...

"There was nothing wrong with the warrant *per se*," the Assistant D.A. who had botched *State of Oklahoma vs. Durwood Durante, et. al* now said. "We had probable cause to search the premises for evidence of prostitution and illegal gambling, but Durante's a slippery con artist. He engaged a deputy sheriff in friendly conversation and…"

Yeah, the devilishly devious club owner/operator had voluntarily conducted a veritable V.I.P. tour of the den, pointing out and describing incriminating evidence of criminal enterprise and even signing a statement introduced at this morning's pre-trial heaingr as his confession, but…

Damnit, by his nonstop patter the master of deception had distracted the deputy sheriff from first reciting a so-called *"Miranda* Warning" that he had a right to remain silent and a right to assistance of counsel. By application of the Exclusionary Rule, the confession, plus—per the so-called Poison Tree Doctrine—other evidence gathered as a result, had been ruled inadmissible by old Judge Dwight before his adjournment to tomorrow of the hearing on the Prosecution's motion for a Cease-and-Desist Order against Durante.

Rationale for the Rule was that not allowing improperly obtained evidence to be used against a defendant—even at the cost of an obviously guilty evil doer beating a rap—was necessary in order to deter investigative tactics by law enforcement officers that violated a perp's constitutional rights. Bullshit. Just another example of bleeding-heart left-wing coddling of criminals, and…

"We argued for an exception to the Rule."his assistant whined. "We argued that the legal search of the premises and the tainted confession were two separate things, and—per the U.S. Supreme Court decision in *Nix v. Williams*—that law enforcement personnel would have found the proffered evidence regardless of defendant's confession. We cited Justice Scalia's opinion in *Hudson v. Michigan* to the effect that the Exclusionary Rule generates substantial social costs and is a last resort; that the toll upon truth-seeking presents a high obstacle for its application; and that the Rule should be held applicable, quote, 'only where its remedial objectives are thought most efficaciously served.'"

Damnit, two wrongs—Durante's vice and prosecutorial "misconduct"—didn't make a right, not in Ham's as yet unwritten book to be titled *Simple As A Ham Sandwich*. The most efficacious common-sensible way to deter an Oklmulgee County deputy sheriff from failing to respect a criminal suspect's constitutional rights would be to not only allow the wronged party to sue the deputy for civil damages, but also require that the deputy be criminally charged for stepping on toes. But Judge Dwight was known for being not the smartest jar of mustard on the shelf. So the Durante "sandwich", though simple...

Hmmm. For effectively—wittingly or not—aiding and abetting Durante's ongoing criminal enterprise, Ham contemplated adding his bungling legal assistant to the list of defendants in in his RICO prosecution, but...

"Sorry to interrupt," said his clerical assistant through an opened crack in the doorway to his office. "Representatives of the SOW are here, and urgently want to see you."

SOW? Oh yeah, the Henryetta Chapter of the Society of Women, a group of nagging do-gooders...

"Ms. Dimwitty says she has new evidence for use in the case against Durwood Durante and his den of iniquity."

During a fund-raising speech at a luncheon meeting of Ms. Dimwitty's organization, Ham had encouraged the brood of hens to—figuratively speaking—stop clucking and start mucking out the sources of vice corrupting weak-minded members of the community. Rhetorically speaking, he had promised his door would always be open to them.

That said—though only figuratively and rhetorically—he now dubiously went from his office into an adjacent conference room, where the elderly SOW leader, already seated between two other women, greeted him with a distinctly disapproving look in her eyes.

"Your so-called RICO case against the Devil seems to be as bogged down as the one that Georgia District Attorney—the notorious Ms. Fani Willis—filed against President Trump," she said. "I hope we will not find that you too have been compromised by surreptitious hanky-panky with your assistant."

Ham ignored the slanderous suggestion and informed the naive old do-gooder that building a complicated RICO case took time and ongoing effort.

"Ha!" she snorted, gingerly nudging a green folder across a table. "In this dossier you will find shocking documentary evidence proving that the Second Circle Club is a house of ill repute, and that its proprietor is the Devil. Oh yes, *Revelations 12:19* expressly identifies Eve's corrupter as 'that ancient serpent called the devil, or Satan, who leads the whole world astray.'"

As he opened the folder…

"Given that you and your staff have failed to muck out that stable of whores tended to by the despicable Durwood 'Damnedest' Durante, we took it upon ourselves to engage the services of a private investigator, namely Mr. Maximo Morgan, and within twenty-four hours…"

Oh no, the overweight Notary Public—a living, breathing caricature of an old-fashioned "private dick"—was well known to county law enforcement personnel as a meddlesome bumbler prone to f'ing up "ham sandwiches". But…

Praise the Lord! Photos inside the folder were in fact shocking evidence of vice, and—if tied to the Second Circle Club—highly incriminating to Durwood "Durndest" Durante.

CHAPTER THREE

In a sweat, Max steered his mom's brown Buick boiler into downtown Okmulgee... found a parking spot... hotfooted across 7th Street... and entered the county courthouse.

To a broad manning the District Attorney's reception desk he explained that he had been summoned by phone to appear this afternoon without fail. Shown into a conference room, he commenced to pace while again mentally rehearsing the story he would stick to.

Dang it, Old Lady Dimwitty was the leader of a so-called Society of Women dedicated to exposing what was described in *Case of The Usual Suspects* documentary as "the Devil's greatest trick": convincing the world that he did not exist. Only because the SOW leader was a member of his mom's Bible study group and... In a nutshell, though Yours Truly was otherwise not affiliated with the Society of Women, a commendable sense of duty to his mom had left him with no choice but to take on the charitable lay of putting a peep on the Second Circle Club.

Yeah, he'd noticed the sign that said only members were allowed to enter the club's inner sanctum through its green door. And no, he was not a member. But he'd made the forgivable mistake of talking the talk to a barroom blonde, and with the lay turned sideways—intending to walk the walk—at the end of a hallway leading to a public Gents room he had come to a door, signed "Manager", not "Exit".

No, he was not a manager, but the door was unlocked and...

"Ah, Mr. Morgan," said a middle-aged dark-suited guy, coming through a doorway into the conference room with... Uh oh, the

District Attorney—Hamilton Burger—recognizable from the many election signs he'd posted in recent years—had in hand a green folder identical to the one into which Ms. Dimwitty had put…

"Have a seat and tell me about these materials that came into your possession," the D.A. said, after sitting down at the table and opening the green folder.

Max lowered his double-wide backside into a tight-fitting chair and recited a slightly expanded account of circumstances leading to his entry into the Manager's office.

"You were 'fleeing' unwelcome advances by a buxom blonde?" said Burger, with a look of disbelief on his kisser. "Did she expressly solicit you to engage in a sexual act in exchange for money?"

"Uh, well, not s-e-x-u-a-l for money, no. But private dicks are chick magnets. It goes with the territory and…"

"What did you do when you 'found' yourself in the club's management office?"

"Nobody was there, so… so like I said, not that I was curious, I just looked around and…"

"Took pictures of a wall-mounted array of naked women in suggestive poses?" said Burger, fumbling through photos in the green folder. "Pictures identifying the women as, let's see," he said, squinting. "'Dido'… 'Cleopatra'… 'Queen Guinevere'… 'Princess Isolde'… someone named 'Francesca da Rimini'… 'Madame Bovary'… 'Fanny Hill'… 'Lady Chatterley'… 'Irma La Douce'… 'Susie Wong'… 'Monica Lewinsky'… and so forth. All names of women famous for engaging in, uh, lustful adventures, I'm told."

"Yours Truly didn't look at any of them," said Max, dripping sweat. "I just took some pictures with my phone and…"

"And picked up these records of payments for services rendered, along with these betting slips, right?"

"Well, yeah, but just to look at, not to…"

"Don't sweat it, Max," said the prosecutor, leaning back in his chair and smiling like cats who ate canaries were said to do. "Given that these materials have no financial value, I'm not inclined to file charges against you."

Phew! What a relief.

"But in connection with another case—a RICO prosecution against Durwood Durante and others involved in a local version of the *Cosa Nostra*—I will need you to testify…"

"Testify in court? No way, José. Yours Truly has no clue about what goes on behind that green door."

"No *problemo*, Max. All you need to tell a judge is that you, a private citizen, uh, came across this evidence after accidentally making a wrong turn along a darkened club hallway into what you mistook as a room for 'Gents'."

But that was a *problemo*, Max complained. His mom would find out that he had been a cat… out late while she was playing Canasta… not just peeping from a distance, but talking to a buxom blonde at the bar while drinking root beer… and that—by accident—he might have caught a gander of the photos of naked women famous for lustful adventures.

CHAPTER FOUR

Willis "Versus" Willis leaned back in his cowhide-covered chair and put his shoeless feet on his rustic office desk... also laden with a half-empty Jim Beam bottle... a recently emptied glass... and a small radio coincidentally tuned into his mood:

♫Once I built a railroad, made it run/ Made it race against time... ♫

In his bygone youth he had wanted to be a farmer, but his mother had a long-standing grudge against a door-to-door salesman who had yoked her with lifetime magazine subscriptions. And so...

♫Once I built a railroad, now it's done/ Brother, can you spare a dime?... ♫

Willis sighed. He had become a country lawyer, plying his craft in the storefront office across the street from the county courthouse in the small county seat town of Okmulgee, Oklahoma. After almost forty years of pettifogging...

♫Once I built a tower to the sun... ♫

Hell's bells, though his middle initial was V-for-Virgil, he had acquired the handle "Versus" for once appearing in court as attorney for both Plaintiff and Defendant in the same contentious case. As the punch line of the old so-called joke explained: divorce was expensive to clients, or used to be, because it was worth it. But damnit, while the county unhitching rate was holding steady at about 35%, the marriage rate was barely more than half of what it was back in 1990. And law schools were cranking out would-be shysters like green grass through a goose.

♫Once I built a tower, now it's done/ Brother, can you spare a dime?... ♫

To boot, divorce cases nowadays tended to be less contentious for the very reason that the usual cause was that not even one could afford to live as cheaply as two used to get by on. With not enough marital assets at stake to support much milking... Hell, these days a country lawyer had a hard time billing fifty or sixty hours for arranging an uncontested one-way trip to Splitsville, not to mention the added chore of collecting the starvation wages he had coming to him for putting asunder the ties that nowadays only loosely bound.

♫Say, don't you remember, they called me Al/ Say, don't you remember, I'm your pal... ♫

As he began to nod off, Willis was startled by the clomping sound of hurried heavy footfalls. He looked up hopefully, but...

♫Brother, can you spare a dime?... ♫

"Sorry to barge in without an appointment," said only Max Morgan. "Yours Truly is in a pickle barrel and in need of a mouthpiece."

Willis straightened up some and turned off the radio used for masking conversations with potentially dissatisfied clients who might be wired.

Morgan was an ex-mailman from the nearby town of Henryetta, who—years ago—had been helpful to finding forwarding addresses for deadbeat husbands. Much to his regret later—when the overweight ex-letter carrier set up shop as "Maximo Morgan, the Fat Man"—he had engaged the newly minted so-called private detective to track down a runaway wife. Morgan was not likely to have a dime in his pocket, but with time on his hands...

"Never too busy to lend a hand to a colleague," said Willis. "Take a load off your feet, Max. Your shoes, and socks too. No need to put on airs in the company of Willis V. Willis, just a country lawyer doin' what I can to help my fellow man out of... pickle barrels."

The "Fat Man" explained that, as an act of charity, he had taken on a private investigation for an also charitable organization of old women who were upset about possible vice going on at the Second Circle Club on the outskirts of Henryetta.

Willis silently noted that working for charity and snooping on Durwood "Durndest" Durante's roadhouse rackets were the first two of what would no doubt prove to be the barrel of missteps. And sure enough...

"Until just now put wise by the District Attorney, I had no idea the... the business establishment I happened to patronize was owned and operated by... For crying out loud, Mr. Durante is reputed to be a clever schemer, an organizer of devious devilry, a criminal mastermind on par with Sherlock Holmes' arch rival, Professor James Moriarty! People say Durante—like Moriarty—is a spider at the center of a web encompassing half of what's evil and nearly all that goes undetected in the entire county!"

As the overweight client continued to squeal like the proverbial stuck pig, Willis was gratified by a sense that what went around came around on the Lazy Susan of of justice. He had sent Christmas hams in payment for prior services rendered by the mailman turned so-called private detective. Now, on the platter in timely repayment, courtesy of Ham Burger...

"I happened to, uh, notice some, uh, things in the club's management office, and happened to... Mr. Burger is not going to file charges against Yours Truly, but wants Yours Truly to testify in court about where I, uh, found the materials. I'd rather not go public about the 'where' part, or about anything else. So since I, uh, happened to be in the neighborhood..."

Hmmm.

In the already much publicized prosecution of Durante under the Oklahoma version of Racketeer Influenced and Corrupt Organization Statute, the District Attorney would have a number of advantages such as put to use by the Georgia D. A.—Fani-no relation-Willis—in her RICO case against Trump and fellow alleged wrongdoers in the 2020 election. To prove a "criminal enterprise" of attempted undoing of election results, the extraneously disgraced prosecutor charged nineteen defendants and lined up a hundred and fifty witnesses to show that a sprawling combination of illegal acts amounted to a criminal conspiracy.

With that number of characters involved, many would have testified to factuall bits and pieces to produce a mosaic of sorts, if only to save themselves from potential criminal liability. And had Fani not "screwed the pooch", so to speak, a big trial would no doubt have been televised.

On the other side of the politically partisan divide, Burger was known to be an also rabidly ambitious politician, and prosecution of "vice" would appeal to a MAGA base of voters. That was what was rolling the barrel Max Morgan was in. Like Democrat Members of the "people's" House of Representatives in Washington proposing legislation to, say, prosecute Trump for spitting on sidewalks, or Republican Members still blowing smoke about putting Biden in the dock, Burger would speechify—and fund-raise—on the moral menace of goings-on at the Second Circle Club. Then quietly settle for a relatively modest fine and softish slap on Durwood Durante's wrist.

Among other considerations, virtually no male in the county would want to have the D.A. risk their names coming up in public criminal litigation involving the notorious "house of ill repute". But...

"You were right as rain to seek legal counsel," said Willis to the worried client. "Hell's bells, Durndest Durante is reputed to be a lowlife who might stop at nothing to keep you from possibly putting him out of bidness and behind bars. Sumbitch might even 'put' back at you by..."

"By putting out a contract?!"

"Not to worry, Max. I'll talk to Burger off the record; try to get him to allow you to take the stand with a sack over your head, heh, heh, and..."

"Oh no! Mom will recognize me by my voice, and pear-shaped physique."

"... afterward, I'll lean on the D.A.—call-in some I.O.U.s

for past favors—and maybe get him to set up enrollment in a witness protection program for both you and your mom."

"OMG!"

"But all that will take a lot of old-fashioned country lawyering, and time is…"

"I'm supposed to testify tomorrow, at a… at continuation of a Cease-and-Desist hearing that is already in progress!"

Uh oh.

Willis was surprised. Ham Burger was dumb, but not stupid. And in addition to the perils of going public, the cagy D.A. would know there was no telling what surprises might and almost always did pop up inside a courtroom. Sadder-but-wiser shell-shocked lawyers—both prosecutors and defense counsel—avoided things blowing up in their faces at all costs, speaking of which…

"Max, you'll need legal representation at the Cease-and-Desist hearing to make sure your rights are protected, but at the moment I'm awful…"

Begged by the client to be at his side for tomorrow's court date… paid a reasonable retainer fee equal to the cost of a boatload of Christmas hams… and left to himself, Willis took his feet off the desk and picked up a phone to call the D.A.s office.

Max Morgan was no doubt a small "pickle" in Burger's RICO case barrel. And in criminal litigation the easy part of old-fashioned country lawyering was getting also risk-averse prosecutors to settle for pleas to lesser offenses and—like members of Congress—declare victory and move on. The hard part was to then persuade clients to take their medicine, and move on.

CHAPTER FIVE

Despite the not-to-worry advice delivered by Willis Willis, Max—back at the wheel of the brown boiler—did worry. And not just about getting in Dutch with his mom. If the country lawyer failed to set the D.A. straight... Dang it, with pedal to the metal in flight to home base, he worried about crossing the now identified owner/ operator of the Second Circle Club—Durwood "Durndest" Durante—the local lord of vice who, like the legendary Professor Moriarty...

In Sherlock Holmes' *Case of The Final Problem*, the not-so-smart British detective—after getting the goods on Moriarty and turning the evidence over to police—fled to Switzerland to escape payback, but was tracked down by the devilish arch villain. According to later case reports, Holmes remained missing in action and presumed dead for three years.

And that case was not Yours Truly's only exposure the risks of being a whistleblower. His long-deceased father's attic cache of pulp case reports documenting the exploits of famous gumshoes dating back to days and murky nights of *Noir* were littered with accounts of witnesses to crimes having to lay low in fear of being bumped off before or after testifying in court. Since his teenaged years, he had also studied numerous film documentaries of such cases handled by countless other private dicks. But... nowadays, heck, under witness protection programs, hiding out had become a commonplace American way of life.

True, many if not most known protectees—such as the Mafia hitman in the famous *Goodfellas Case*—were organized-crime thugs who had ratted out big cheeses. But other cases involved good guys, and gals, notably including the *Sister Act Case* in which a female nightclub singer got put away in a nunnery after witnessing her boyfriend commit murrrderrr. In the animated documentary of a so-called *Cape Feare Case*, the entire Simpson family changed their name to "Thompson" and holed-up in an undisclosed location after an imprisoned mope named Sideshow Bob wrote letters to Bart threatening revenge for his incarceration.

Heck, approximately twenty thousand witnesses and their families were now being officially protected, according to a recent edition of *Private Dick Data*. And according to the U.S. Marshals Service, not a single protected victim had been discovered and harmed. In a SpongeBob SquarePants cartoon-for-kids *Case of The Squidless Protection*, a punk falsely admitted to witnessing a robbery in order to live a <u>better</u> life in witness protection. But... Dang it, most reported cases painted life-on-the-lam as *sub rosy*.

In the Family Guy *Case of To Live and Die In Dixie*, for instance, the family of a witness to a robbery was forced to relocate from a pleasant hometown to a backwater community of rednecks waving Confederate flags and shotguns. And in almost all other cases on record, protectees lived in constant fear of being accidentally spotted, if not identified by leakage of government information, and/or—like the *Goodfellas Case* wiseguy—dying of boredom.

So yeah, as he entered downtown Henryetta, Max worried that if Willis Willis was not otherwise able to get him out of testifying against Durante, Yours Truly—like a trapped rat, so to speak—might have to chew off his testicles, so to speak, to avoid being tracked down by scent and whacked.

Parking the boiler at the curb out front of Mister Quickie's copy shop, he was overcome with dread at the prospect of having to live under a fake name in some out-of-the-way location, working as, say, an ordinary store clerk—if not a nun—to avoid recognition.

Entering the copy shop and ankling toward the workstation cubicle that served as his office, he shuddered at the thought of

his real self, faced with having to chew off… as disappeared…
still technically alive but likely reported dead.

Inside the cubicle… Hello, seated in the client chair was
the teenaged kid who served as his case report jotter, like Doc
Watson did for Sherlock Holmes.

To the also pear-shaped kid — a wannabe private dick — Yours
Truly was a role model for his ambition to someday walk in
his own gumshoes. And though still green behind the ears,
his young protege had also studied most if not all of the pulp
and film records of cases handled by famous private dicks, plus
occasionally passed on useful tips from one of his uncles, a rabbi.

So after plopping his own over-sized buttocks into his
double-wide chair…

"Gee, Mr. Max, you look sorta green around the gills."

Barely into an account of his pickle-barrel predicament…

"The District Attorney is prosecuting Mr. Durwood and a
gang of thugs from Costa Rica?" said the kid.

"Yeah, and wants Yours Truly to testify against the lord of
organized crime about what I detected at the Second Circle
Club."

"I think you must mean the D.A. is prosecuting the reputed
crime boss under the RICO law."

RICO?

"Racketeer Influenced and Corrupt Organization, Mr. Max.
Back in the day, Mr. Rudy Giuliani busted the *Cosa* — not
Costa — *Nostra* a/k/a Mafia crime syndicate when he was a U.S.
Attorney, and went on to become 'America's Mayor'."

"Yeah, whatever. I was a little nervous at the time about the
D.A. wanting Yours Truly to be a whistleblower."

"Rightly so, Mr. Max. Remember what happened to Jimmy
Altiera when Tony Soprano found out he had ratted out the
Jersey mob to the Feds."

"Witness protection?"

"Witness toes up."

More nervous, Max put his young protege wise to the story
he'd decided not to stick to.

"You sneaked into a private office?" said the kid in a holier-than-him tone of voice. "Gee, Mr. Max, even if Mr. Durante is guilty of promoting vice, that was a violation of his constitutional right to do it secretly."

"I didn't even look at the photos… and the financial records I happened to pick up have no value. Wise up, kid. If you're ever gonna cut the mustard as a private dick, you're gonna have to learn to cut corners. Heck, Father Brown, a man of cloth, has a handy gadget on his key ring and picks locks in almost every case he handles."

"And you turned over the ill-gotten evidence to authorities, right?"

"Yeah, indirectly. And then it was my civic duty to come clean about my, uh, accidental visit to Durante's office, which just goes to show: no good deed goes unpunished. Now the D.A. expects Yours Truly to testify in court, but…"

"Good for you, Mr. Max. Do you suppose Mr. Quickie would let me set up shop in the cubicle when you disappear into witness protection?"

That did it. No way, no how was Yours Truly vacating the big chair, no matter what. He was, okay, a curious cat, not a rat, and…

"Don't count any chickens, kid. Yours Truly is not gonna dress up like a nun and move to Mississippi or anywhere else."

"Hanging around would be risky, Mr. Max. As Uncle Ralph would likely say, the better part of valor would be to lay low, and let me sit in for you, just for a while until…"

"Durante will have no beef with Yours Truly. As put by Charlie Chan in *Case of Three Wise Monkeys*, 'Speak no evil', which means a guy should mind his own business."

"Not testify? But… But… But… Mr. Max, you have already butted into monkey business at the Second Circle Club. You've uncovered evidence of evil. By not testifying you will allow Durante to go on promoting vice."

" Silence is Golden, that's the Golden Rule."

"But… But… But… While it was wrong of you to snoop,

as Uncle Ralph would say: two wrongs don't make a right, Mr. Maximo."

"Yours Truly already has a right," Max snapped, "The United States Constitution guarantees right to life, liberty and… Dang it, pursuit of happiness is the sacred Law of the Land!"

TUESDAY

July 22, 2025

CHAPTER SIX

♫ Three wise monkeys' golden rule/ Looking the other way/ Pretending you're a fool/ 'Cause you don't wanna play… ♫

On the road again, Max felt guilty. Unable to reach Willis Willis for confirmation that the country lawyer had nailed down a waiver of his court date, he'd told his mom he needed the boiler for a drive to Okmulgee on an errand, which was true, but…

♫ The first little monkey keeps his hands over his eyes so tight/ If he doesn't look for anything wrong, he'll see everything is right… ♫

Asked by Mom what the errand was about, he'd semi-fibbed that he needed to drop by the county courthouse to check some documents on file, but…

♫ The second little monkey keeps his hands over his ears so tight/ If he doesn't hear anything wrong, he'll hear everything that's right… ♫

Okay, when Mom hinted—only hinted—that she might like to tag along and do some shopping, he had pretended not to hear. He was guilty of only omission.

♫ The third little monkey keeps his hands over his mouth so tight/ If he doesn't say anything is wrong, he'll say everything is right… ♫

But dang it—despite the kid's whining that "two wrongs don't make a right," he did <u>not</u> feel guilty about <u>not</u> testifying at a hearing on charges that the notorious Durwood "Durndest" Durante had promoted illegal behavior at his Second Circle Club.

Yours Truly had no dog in the fight. Only Ms. Dimwitty was het up about alleged vice afoot. He had simply helped an old lady cross a street, so to speak, without knowledge of what he was doing and/or understanding of what she would do with the work product <u>confidentially</u> handed over to her. For all Yours Truly knew, the Society of Women had just wanted to look at the dirty pictures.

And despite the D.A. putting an arm on him, Willis V. Willis, ani attorney-at-law—to whom he had already made out a check for $1,000—had told him not to worry.

♫ *Three little monkeys swung on a tree/ Teasing Mr. Crocodile, "You can't catch me"*... ♫

Max entered downtown Okmulgee... parked the boiler at the curb on Seventh Street... hotfooted down a sidewalk. but... At Willis Willis" storefront office... IN COURT, said a crudely-lettered sign stuck on the front door, BACK AT 10:30.

It was now 9:45, and the hearing in the case of *State of Oklahoma v. Durwood Durante, et al* was scheduled to resume at 10:00. So the country lawyer was likely not in court to represent Yours Truly. But... Back at 10:30? Would the hearing be over by then? Or was the sign a sign that Willis wouldn't have to be there because he had talked the D.A. into excusing Yours Truly?

Hmmm.

Would it be safe for Yours Truly to enter the courthouse without benefit of counsel at his side, or... ?

♫ *Along came the croc as quiet as could be/ And snatched the little monkey right out of the tree!*... ♫

Hmmm.

Max ducked into a handy coffee shop and... five minutes later exited the joint with a brown paper sack over his head, provided by a jolly waitress, who—before he noticed—had drawn a large, round, bright red nose and bright red-lipped smile beneath the eye-holes she cut out. Not the nondescript look he was going for but...

He ankled across the street... entered the courthouse... and again at the D.A.'s reception desk... crossed his fingers and asked a broad on duty if anyone named Max Morgan was still expected to be a witness at the ten o' clock Cease-and-Desist hearing. She looked down at what looked to be a list, then looked up with a bright smile on her kisser, and...

"To make it official, here's the paperwork," said the record keeper, handing him a folded sheet of paper.

Max unfolded the official document and, uh, oh, instead of a waiver of court appearance…

STATE OF OKLAHOMA

Greetings:

You are commanded to appear before the Honorable Judge Timothy Dwight of the District Court of Okmulgee County on July 22, 2025 at 10:00 a.m. and remain in attendance on call of said Court from day to day and term to term until lawfully discharged, to testify in a criminal action prosecuted by the State of Oklahoma against Durwood Durante, *et al.*

Dang!

With the song about three wise monkeys continuing to echo inside his bean, Max hightailed from the reception area… down a flight of stairs… into a hallway leading to courtrooms.

From prior court appearances as a private dick semi-officially involved in law enforcement, he had professional cred with Judge Dwight, an irritable old coot with a reputation for not suffering for fools. If Willis had bypassed the D.A. and was now in private chambers with the judge, chances of Yours Truly getting off the hook…

♫ *Truth is blind, my mouth is sealed/ Justice kneels, she bows and yields…* ♫

CHAPTER SEVEN

At a table set in the well of Judge Dwight's courtroom, Ham Burger eyed his prey: Durwood Durante... a man into his mid-sixties... unusually tall... gaunt... standing with rounded shoulders... his gray-haired head slowly oscillating in a curiously reptilian way as he chatted with his incompetent local attorney, Old Tom Mashburn.

Also now standing beside the sleazy owner/ operator of the Second Circle Club was a diminutive, dark-haired lawyer from Oklahoma City, Morton P. Fisher, well known mouthpiece for pinheaded causes pushed by the American Civil Liberties Union.

Ham licked his chops as...

"All rise!" a bailiff commanded. "The District Court of Okmulgee County is now in session. Honorable Judge Timothy Dwight presiding."

A black curtain opened behind an elevated perch and — like a county fair magician versed in tricks to befuddle and impress an audience of yokels — the black-robed judge appeared.

"Oyez! Oyez! Oyez! All persons having business before the Court are admonished to draw near and give their attention, for the Court is now sitting in the matter of State of Oklahoma vs. Durwood Durante, *et al.*"

But before His Honor had seated himself in his high chair and taken gavel in hand...

"Your Honor, if I may," said Durante's new co-counsel, short in stature but now up on his toes, obviously eager to spout. "I am Morton P. Fisher, a licensed member of the bar, appearing today on behalf of both the Defendant and our mutual friend, Bill — the

Bill of Rights—otherwise known as the first ten amendments to the Constitution of the United States of America. In that dual capacity, I hereby demand that Your Honor disrobe in this matter, part the curtain, and return to chambers due to…"

Bang! went the judge's gavel, followed by delivery of a silent, steely gaze at the ACLU activist.

Morton P. Fisher's involvement would inevitably both prolong the Cease-and-Desist hearing, and generate notoriety. No doubt Fisher and the ACLU also didn't give a damn about the fate of "Durndest" Durante and the Second Circle brothel-*cum*-casino *per se*, but in the higher court of public opinion…

"In fact, I ruled against admission of evidence against Mr. Durante in the prior session of this hearing," the judge was saying to the feisty outside agitator, "due to violation of the Defendant's constitutional rights by law enforcement personnel investigating his activities. In short, this Court has already demonstrated absence of bias against your client."

"Motion to dismiss the charges," Fisher shot back, "with prejudice," meaning with finality. "This so-called 'continuation' of a Cease-and-Desist hearing allows the State to have a second bite of the apple in gross violation of the Fifth Amendment to the United States Constitution that—in addition to providing that no person shall be compelled to be a witness against himself—further provides that, quote: 'nor shall any person subject to the same offense be twice put in jeopardy of life and limb'."

"Your Honor, if I may," said Ham. "The Supreme Court has ruled that the Fifth Amendment protects against prosecution, not for the same <u>behavior</u> but for the same <u>offense</u>."

"All one ball of wax in a RICO case," Fisher countered. "Allegation of a balled-up ongoing act of promoting illegal activities, for which the Defendant has already been…"

"Your Honor, as constantly reminded by CNN and *The New York Times*," said Ham, with a sidewise glance at the gallery of observers, "President Trump was charged with and convicted of <u>thirty-four</u> separate felonies for—as seldom detailed by media—signing eleven checks and authorizing twenty-three corresponding bookkeeping entries in connection with settlement of a single ongoing blackmail demand by a single porn star."

"Noted," said the judge.

"I would also point out," said Ham, "that this Defendant, while previously charged per standard criminal procedure, has not been tried—nor even bound-over for trial on charges of any offenses he committed—thanks to Your Honor's suppression of his confession to undermining the morals of this community on grounds that Durante—though sporting a criminal record that would make Satan blush—had not been made to understand his so-called *Miranda* rights to remain silent and have benefit of counsel during search of his den of iniquity that would make Satan envious."

"The Court is well aware of its prior ruling and, thanks to the State's reminder, perhaps Sean Hannity will take notice."

"Let's hope so, Your Honor. Since the Court's loosing of the Defendant upon the community yesterday, other evidence..."

"Objection to the District Attorney plucking Fruit of the Poison Tree!" Fisher shouted. "Per numerous Supreme Court decisions, 'other evidence' derived from evidence previously obtained in violation of a Defendant's constitutional rights is tainted fruit, not fit for consumption in a court of law. In layman's terms—to quote words famously spoken by the late President Reagan to the late Queen Elizabeth—'Don't eat that, Lady; it's horseshit.'"

"The Exclusionary Rule is not absolute," Ham contended in reply. "Even in the landmark 1920 case of *Silverthorne Lumber Company v. United States* the Supreme Court—though upholding a lower court exclusion of ill-gotten evidence—pointedly noted that 'facts obtained improperly do not become sacred and inaccessible'. And in recent years, the High Court—led by Justice Alito—has become increasingly reluctant to punch get-out-of-jail-free tickets for the likes of this Defendant."

"Alito was appointed by Bush, and his wife hoisted an ani-

LGBQT flag at their residence," Fisher noted with a smirk, as though that sacred fact settled the constitutional law issue related to criminal procedure.

The facts in support of the current charges against Durante were not accessed by squeezing juice from poisoned fruit, Ham averred. "Neither the D.A.'s Office, nor the County Sheriff, nor any other law enforcement agency authorized the means by which the evidence to be presented by the State in this hearing was obtained. A private citizen stumbled upon the sordid traces of the more rightly forbidden fruit with which Durante satanically tempts the good, God-fearing citizens of Okmulgee County."

"Objection to pollution of these proceedings with unconstitutional religious notions, Your Honor! At an ACLU-sponsored forum on 'Just Say No to the Opiate of the Masses', the eminent constitutional scholar — Professor Lawrence Tribble of the Harvard Law School — authoritatively opined that mere mention of Garden-of-Eden goings-on in a public place violates both the Constitution's Equal Protection Clause for women in special need of protection, and the Separation of Church and State Clause for men with better things to do on Sundays."

Uh oh, Judge Dwight, well known to be an avid weekend golfer, had once publicly said, presumably in jest, that his church absences were required by the Constitution. But the ACLU — like MSNBC commentators — didn't get jesting and…

"On behalf of the American Civil Liberties Union," Fisher continued, "I am currently suing the State Department of Education in this same court to establish that mere presence of a Bible on school grounds clearly calls for application of the Exclusionary Rule to eliminate any and all suggestion that Judeo-Christian religion is or ever was a factor in history and culture fit to be taught in school.

"I am also proud to say that the ACLU's six years of litigation in the case of *Felix v. Bloomfield* — in which I myself was honored to participate — successfully supported the high priestess of the Bloomfield, New Mexico Wiccan coven in her quest to force removal of a five-foot-high granite monument that displayed the biblical Ten Commandments. In other words, Your Honor, the Supreme Court has spoken on proper application of the First Amendment's prescribed separation of church and state that does not allow mention of..."

Ham pointed out that the Supreme Court would have spoken in its courtroom that itself displayed a sculptural depiction of Moses handing down the Ten Commandments.

"Only the first six rules of secular nature are visible behind Moses' beard!" the ACLU pinhead pointed out.

Bang!

"Speaking of Supreme Court interpretations of the Constitution," said Judge Dwight, "I am inclined to side with the Defendant by preemptively applying the 'Exclusionary Rule'..."

Ham winced. Fisher beamed.

"... to you personally, Mr. Fisher, in order to assure that Mr. Durante will not be incompetently represented by counsel in violation of his rights under the Sixth Amendment."

Fisher winced. Ham beamed.

CHAPTER EIGHT

Cowering in the back row of the courtroom's so-called gallery, Max waited with bated breath for Judge Dwight to drop the hammer, but... Minutes passed and... Instead of terminating the hearing, the old man in the black robe now looked to be dropping his jaw... not in surprise but as he nodded off.

The back-and-forth of lawyers must have become boring to the veteran judge. And now—in legalese as incomprehensible as Chinese instructions on a box containing a high-tech gadget—Durante's own two lawyers were going at each other in heated dispute about which of the two of them was too incompetent to satisfy the Defendant's constitutional right to be represented by effective counsel. If Judge Dwight woke up, still tired of the tedious ongoing argle-bargle...

"Is this seat taken?" said a heavyset joker, standing in an aisle and apparently referring to the seat at the end of the bench occupied by Yours Truly. In that spot the guy would be a stumbling block to a possibly urgent need to make a hasty exit, but...

To avoid a face-off that would draw attention to himself. Max scooted over to make room.

"With both Ol' Tom Mashburn and this new guy from Oklahoma City lawyerin' for him, well, Durante's fix reminds me of what they say about Ol' Buddy Hayden," said the pushy stranger. "When my partner and I got called in to identify a body suspected of being the remains of our close friend, there was a corpse lying face down at the scene. But we immediately knew it wasn't Buddy. Know why?"

Max shrugged to signal lack of interest, but…

"'Cause every time the three of us had been out and about people would say, 'Here comes that guy with the two anuses'. Ha, ha, ha…"

Max didn't see the humor, but…

"What do you call one dead lawyer, huh? A good start, right," the joker explained. "So what do you call Durndest Durante's two lawyers? One too many assholes. Ha, ha, ha…"

"The State calls to the stand Ms. Lela Dimwitty."

A tall silver-haired dude, wearing what looked to be an expensive suit of clothes, escorted the elderly Society of Women chairperson into the so-called well of the courtroom and introduced himself as her counsel. The old gal got into the witness box and swore on a Bible that she would tell the whole truth. As the District Attorney approached her, Max nervously shifted his weight from one buttock to the other, but…

As the D.A. began to gently put questions to the witness, he began to relax.

"Here to anonymously testify against Durante?" the nosy stranger seated next to him asked, which was alarming. "Sack over your head tipped me off," the sharp-eyed courtroom kibitzer explained, before sticking out a hand and introducing himself as Pete "Hot Dog" Frank, Attorney-at-Law.

"Got a mouthpiece?" he then asked. "You're gonna need one if you get caught between 'Hammerin' Ham' Burger and those two lawyers blowing smoke for Durante."

In a lowered voice, Max told that he already had a lawyer, and was waiting for Willis Willis to arrive and confirm that Yours Truly would not be called to testify.

"Ol' Willis setting foot inside a courtroom? I wouldn't count on it if I was in your shoes. Willis is a good ol' boy and could bust a move back in the day, they say. But has shot himself in an unquick foot too many times on the dance floor. Now suffers from defense counsel PTSD. Has a hard time just getting out of bed, much less get up the nerve to go toe-to-toe against both that ACLU hired gun and—when the dance step changes from push to shove — do the do-si-do with Hammerin' Ham."

Dang!

"For a modest fee, I would be willing to be your mouthpiece, on one strict condition: your mouth stays shut tighter than a mule's anus in fly season. Put in legal terms: when called to testify in court, the smart play is always to take the Fifth."

Hmmm.

Politicians put under oath — such as Hillary Clinton, once named a Top 100 Lawyer in the U.S. — got away with claiming they could not recall virtually anything they had ever seen, heard, said or done. But according to the many case reports and documentaries he'd studied, other than President Trump, only mobsters — fearful of retaliation for ratting out organized crime bosses — took the Fifth.

"You're likely to find yourself in the same boat, my friend. To avoid being torpedoed your only hope will be to repeatedly say, under oath: 'On advice of counsel, I invoke my constitutional right to not risk self-incrimination, and respectfully decline to answer questions or otherwise provide information.' Then leave the lip service to me."

Hmmm.

Having already paid a grand to Willis Willis for legal lip service, Max visually scanned the courtroom for sight of the country lawyer as...

"When you say the so-called 'Society of Women' is a 'civic-minded' group, what you mean is that SOW is a 'sovereign citizen' group'," the short, dark-haired big-city lawyer was saying to Ms. Dimwitty, "part of the so-called Posse Comiatus Movement like, say, the so-called Washitaw Nation that abides by only so-called 'natural law' administered by it own courts... issues its own car tags... imposes its own fines and..."

"My car tags, yes, they identify me with SOW, but were issued by the State of Oklahoma as so-called vanity plates," the old gal answered. "Our purpose is not to overthrow, but to maintain..."

"Ah yes, when you claim to be concerned with maintenance of western 'civilization', what you really mean is that your organization—like the notorious so-called 'Proud Boys'—is plotting to overthrow the American way of life by spreading hateful white nationalism. Isn't that the real truth?"

"Why no, the American way of life is rooted in western civilization, and in part dependent on a healthy sense of nationalism. Our group hopes to maintain traditional values of…"

"Traditional imperialistic values of expropriating lands of indigenous peoples?" the ACLU mouthpiece screeched. "Traditional racist values of enslaving people of non-white skin color? Traditional capitalistic values of exploiting the honest labor of blue-collar working people? Traditional values of restricting so-called foreigners from establishing their native ways of life in place of American so-called 'patriotism'?"

"Objection, your honor," said the old lady's tall lawyer. "Counsel is badgering the witness, and violating her constitutional rights by implying…"

"I am not 'implying' anything, Your Honor. In defense of Mr. Durante's rights under multiple clauses of the Bill of Rights, I am expressly bringing to the Court's attention that this fascist fox in granny clothes sneaked into a private citizen's hen house and illegally obtained evidence that must be ruled inadmissible in this and any other proceeding."

"Your Honor, the State objects to defense Counsel's line of cross-examination that serves only to smear the reputation of this good private citizen, a legally protected whistleblower who had the courage to pucker-up and blow."

"I never did, and would never set foot in that den of debauchery!" Ms. Dimwitty protested. "The filthy photos and other incriminating materials were discovered by a private, uh, citizen and brought to my attention."

"Oh? Who is this Proud Boy or Proud Girl who breached the Defendant's Fourth Amendment rights to be secure in his person, papers, and den of debauchery?!"

Max shifted weight to a single buttock…

"As I said, he is a private… person, who requested that I keep our dealings confidential."

… then shifted weight to the other one.

"Make her spill her guts!" the ACLU lawyer shrieked. And though his shaken fist failed to land… Uh oh, Old Lady Dimwitty slumped, then slid from the witness box onto the courtroom floor.

Ohhhhh others in the gallery moaned.

"Is there a doctor in the house?!" the District Attorney shouted.

"Throw a bucket of water on her!" Fisher urgently urged.

"The Court is hereby in recess!" the judge declared.

Bang!

Phew! Max was relieved.

Ms. Dimwitty—though now sprawled unconscious at the ACLU lawyer's feet—had proved to be a stand-up broad. And by taking the fall for Yours Truly's possibly unkosher visit to Durwood Durante's disreputable Second Circle Club office, yeah, the SOW leader had thwarted undue process of law by the D.A. in violation of Yours Truly's constitutional right to be a blind, deaf and, not "dumb", but wisely non-speaking monkey.

CHAPTER NINE

Willis opened an eye, then another.

An empty bottle on a table beside the cot in his office—along with a headache—reminded him that he had over-indulged in the company of Jim Beam last night. A clock further informed him that it was now 10:30 a.m. Semi-recalling that he had come back to the office at a wee hour... had posted a reminder somewhere about an appointment and... Oh yeah, in dreadful anticipation of arriving for work and having to make an early courtroom appearance, he had put a sign on the door to announce he would be back by... by now!

Willis sat upright... got his feet into a pair of slip-ons... ran fingers through his hair... and hurried from the storefront office. No harm, no foul, he muttered to himself. Additional grooming would suggest he indulged in a refined and expensive lifestyle—supported by excessive fees—inappropriate for a country lawyer.

And by the time he had hustled across the street... entered the county courthouse... and made his way to the main courtroom... he was barely tardy for a pre-hearing chat with Ham Burger about not calling Max Morgan to the stand in the Cease-and-Desist hearing related to RICO charges against Durwood Durante.

Judge Dwight—probably also running late due to a back-up of early birds on a golf course—had not yet taken the bench. Standing in the well of the courtroom, Burger was just now sorting papers and...

"Oyez!" the bailiff bellowed. "The District Court of Okmulgee

County is back in session, Judge Dwight presiding."

Willis stumbled into the well, but…

"The State calls Max Morgan to the stand," the D.A. hollered.

… as he visually searched the gallery for presence of his client…

"Peter Frank, Esquire, appearing on behalf of the witness," said Hot Dog Frank, barging into the well by mistake.

"Willis V. Willis, country lawyer, appearing on behalf of Max Morgan, Your Honor. If the Court would allow me a moment to, uh, locate and consult with my client…"

"Mr. Morgan is _my_ client, Your Honor," said Frank. "I have already located and consulted with him and…"

"Objection, Your Honor!" the D.A. barked. "I don't mind being double-teamed by dueling mouthpieces for the Defendant, but to waste time dealing separately with Tweedle Dee and Tweedle Dum reprenting the witness…"

"I am Mr. Morgan's _co_-counsel," said Willis, seizing upon the opportunity to get himself off a hook, "and gladly defer to my colleague to speak for both of us on our client's behalf."

"To avoid waste of time," Frank continued, "I was about to apprise the Court in advance that if required to take the stand, Mr. Morgan, on advice of counsel, will take the Fifth and respectfully decline to answer any and all questions put to him by the District Attorney."

Ohhh gallery onlookers ohhhed.

Though Judge Dwight looked expectantly in the direction of the Durante's lawyers — virtually winking to signal he would favorably entertain a motion to dismiss the D. A.'s Cease-and-Desist motion for failure of Burger to produce evidence — the two Defense attorneys remained oddly silent.

"Let's hear the witness deny under oath what he previously had to say," said Burger, seizing the opening. And the judge, with a sigh of obvious reluctance, agreed.

Wearing a brown paper sack over his head, with a smily face drawn on it, a fat man — presumably Max Morgan — took the stand, swore to tell the whole truth, and in fact "took the Fifth".

But then explained that he did so only on advice of counsel and, uh oh, "not because Yours Truly is a politician or mobster afraid to rat out Mr. Durante."

Ohhh…

Willis bit his tongue, so to speak, or rather so not to speak. Already exposed as a witness technically "hostile" to the Prosecution, the gabby gumshoe—by carelessly testifying to incidental facts—had opened the door to otherwise prohibited leading questions by the D.A. on cross-examination. And sure enough…

"Not afraid to 'rat out' the Defendant, you say?" said Burger, pouncing like a proverbial rooster on a proverbial June bug. "And not afraid to undertake a private investigation of Mr. Durante's illicit business enterprises on behalf of the Society of Women, concerned about his operation of a den of iniquity right out of Sodom and Gomorrah, right?"

Ohhh…

"Well, like I say, on advice of Counsel…"

Again oddly, old Tom Mashburn and his co-counsel didn't object on behalf of Durwood.

"Not afraid to patronize the Defendant's so-called Second Circle Club and entertain solicitation for sex in return for money by at least one of Defendant's employees, right?"

Ohhh…

"Well, like I say…"

"Not afraid to stumble down a hallway in search of a urinal and accidentally open an unlocked door to the Defendant's office, right?"

"Well…"

Ha! As Willis himself had done on numerous prior occasions, the District Attorney was using the witness as a prop for a theatrical performance—not unlike those staged by congressional committee members—designed not to elicit answers, but to effectively introduce evidence in the form of leading questions, not for deliberation by the trial judge but for voters in the politically higher court of public opinion. And lawyers for the Defendant, it now seemed, might be similarly motivated to have a "show trial" of sorts to score points for political causes.

In the process, Morgan had already skated perilously close to inadvertently waiving his Fifth Amendment rights, and in fact incriminating himself.

"Not afraid to come upon photographs of unclothed females in suggestive poses, along with other documentary evidence of Durante's engagement in pimping prostitution and promoting illegal gambling. Right, Mr. Morgan?"

Ohhh...

"I never even looked at the dirty pictures. I was afraid my mom would..."

"But not afraid to turn over the evidence of Durante's vile wrongdoing to the Society of Women, knowing that the group of concerned 'non-sovereign' citizens would..."

As the short, dark-haired attorney at the Defense table rose to his feet with a "gotcha" look in his eyes...

"Would you mind repeating the question that I refuse to answer?" said Max.

Fearful of being found guilty himself, by association in incompetent lawyering...

"Your Honor, please pardon my prior mistake, "said Willis, "and accept my, uh, disappearance on behalf of the witness. As the old joke about Buddy Hayden goes, a client with two attorneys is like a man with..."

"The Court is not amused!" Judge Dwight declared. "But 'disappearance' granted. Get out of the well, Mr. Willis."

Bang!

CHAPTER TEN

Feeling pretty darn proud of himself, Max took off the brown paper sack that had concealed his face. Okay, not his body size-and-shape, voice… and name, but no *problemo*. By exercising his right to not testify against Mr. Durante, he had stood up for the Second Circle Club owner/operator's right not to have his office searched.

So win-win. Balled together, their two rights had effectively canceled the alleged "wrong" of Yours Truly's investigation, and eliminated reason for Durante to retaliate. Blinded justice had been served. But as he stepped out…

"Get back in the box!" Durante's big-city mouthpiece commanded. "I have a few 'questions' of my own to put on the public record, to-wit:

"Mr. Morgan, as a highly trained and licensed private investigator, you no doubt flashed your credentials upon entering the Second Circle Club on Friday night, right?"

"Well, no, I was working undercover as a highly trained and licensed gumshoe."

"You took a five-dollar bill from your wallet and unsuccessfully attempted to bribe your way into a Members Only section of the club premises, right?"

"Well, sorta. But not because I was <u>sinfully</u> curious about what was going on behind a green door. I just wondered …"

"And did you in fact find out what was going behind closed doors after making a surreptitious rear entry?"

"Well, depending on what you mean by surreptious 'rear entry'…"

"Did you 'by chance' find that many of this community's leading citizens were enjoying themselves in fellowship as they, perhaps, sang hymns, engaged in Bible study, and exercised their right to silent prayer in a non-public place?"

"No, I never got into the red-dotted forbidden-fruit stand. I only found a back door to a manager's office, practically already open, and…"

"And inside a private office you 'happened to notice' photos of women in states of undress, representing to your dirty mind what you <u>suspected</u> was 'going on behind that green door', where—for all you actually <u>knew</u>—the Mayor's Missus was down on her knees."

Ohhh…

"The Mayor doesn't have a Missus, but yeah, after meeting a buxom blonde at the public bar earlier, I glanced—barely glanced—at the photos you mentioned. Putting two-and-two together and coming up with…"

"Coming up with zero, zilch, nada, nothing that is <u>admissible</u> as evidence of wrongdoing by the Defendant, Mr. Durante," said the feisty lawyer from Oklahoma City, not to Yours Truly but to Judge Dwight.

"Your Honor, while the D.A. would have the Court believe that Mr. Morgan acted as a private citizen to assist a legitimate 'whistleblower', evidence illegally obtained via searches by even private citizens is disallowed by multiple court decisions if such searches are made under color of law.

"And the witness admits that he—a licensed detective, well known in the community as a former uniformed member of the United States Postal Service—acted on behalf of a so-called 'Society of Women' whose avowed objective to maintain traditional values of western civilization is consistent with those of the so-called 'Proud Boys' who attacked the U.S. Capitol on January 6th."

Ohhhhh…

"Thus, any and all evidence obtained by this 'Proud Boy's' actions under color of albeit pseudo-law—regardless of its probative content and no less than if illegally seized by the local Sheriff or the F.B.I.—must be viewed per the time-honored Exclusionary Rule—or rather, not viewed—with a blind eye."

Ohhh...

"Though not necessarily in agreement with Counsel's characterization of SOW—my Missus is a member—the Court is inclined to agree with Counsel," said the judge, taking hammer in hand.

Oh...

"In addition," Durante's pesky mouthpiece continued, "given that this is effectively a second hearing on essentially the same charges against my client, and that the District Attorney is no doubt already in possession of 'Fruit of the Poison Tree' by the bushel—with intent to cherry-pick more—Defendant again moves for dismissal of the State's demand for Cease-and-Desist, with prejudice to assure that his Sixth Amendment right to not be subjected to double jeopardy is protected."

Ohhh...

"So ordered! No Cease-and-Desist prior to trial of the Defendant in the State's case in-chief."

Bang!

Though disappointed that protection of his and Durante's rights would no doubt result in undesisted vice at the Second Circle Club, Max got up from the courtroom hot seat with a sense of renewed relief. But...

"Your Honor," said the District Attorney, "before adjournment, we might as well tend to a loose end of this ball of yarn while involved parties are present."

"I'm listening."

"The State hereby adds Max Morgan to the *et als* of its RICO case in-chief, and will demand that the Court impose a penalty of not less than five years in prison, payment of a fine of not less than five thousand dollars, and that he be held without bail pending trial."

Max collapsed into the hotter witness box seat, and...

The judge directed a fish-eye at Ham Burger, but...

"He's confessed to the essential facts," said the D.A.

Judge Dwight turned a fishier eye onto Yours Truly.

Dang it, Burger had promised to not file charges against him, but... but... but... Okay, Yours Truly had more or less agreed to testify against Durwood Durante, but... but... but... For a one thousand-dollar fee, Willis V. Willis had failed to get him out of the pickle barrel, and... and... and... Okay, he'd taken the Fifth — but on advice of new counsel — and had a constitutional right to answer the D.A.'s questions without incriminating himself. Despite all that legal maneuvering...

"Your Honor," said Willis V. Willis, returning to the courtroom well with a hand held up, "permission requested to reappear on behalf of Mr. Morgan regarding the charges newly lodged against him."

"Make it quick and to the point," the judge ordered.

"I have just one question for Mr. Burger," said the country lawyer, wheeling to face the D.A. "Prior to Max Morgan confessing his involvement in matters related to investigation of local vice, did you apprise him of his so-called *Miranda* rights to remain silent and have counsel present?"

Ohhh...

"No *Miranda* warning was called for," the D.A. answered. "I simply recited a statement of facts provided by Ms. Dimwitty, and Morgan — a veteran 'law enforcement official', as noted by Mr. Fisher — chose to confirm them. Until his appearance in today's proceeding, I had no intent to file charges."

Oh...

Max again awaited announcement of his fate with bated breath, but...

"Your Honor, dismissal of the charge against this Proud Boy would be an egregious wrong," said Durante's mouthy mouthpiece, butting in like one of those yappy little foreign terrier mutts originally bred to harass rats out of holes in the ground. "As previously noted, Morgan is a licensed detective engaged in pseudo-law enforcement. To ignore his confession under *Miranda* and the Exclusion Rule would be asinine."

With a set jaw and glint in the eye, Judge Dwight again raised his gavel and…

"As a matter of law, I do not disagree," said the judge.

Oh no. Here it came: blinded injustice for Yours Truly.

"Your Honor, upon reconsideration of the matter in the light of Mr. Fisher's astute big-city lawyering, the Defense for Mr. Morgan concedes that the District Attorney may not have violated his *Miranda* rights," said Willis Willis. "Therefore…"

Dang it, though not a "rat—he had taken the Fifth, for crying out loud—Max realized he was caught in a trap: being ganged-up on by both the D.A. and Durante's het-up lawyer, and being misrepresented by an incompetent mouthpiece probably intent on currying favor with the District Attorney and getting an I.O.U. for future use in another case.

"… with regard to proper application of the time-honored Exclusionary Rule," Willis was saying, "as bemoaned by the eminent jurist, Judge Cardozo in *People v. Defoe*: 'The criminal is to go free because the constable has blundered.'"

"Counsel has just now conceded that the District Attorney did <u>not</u> 'blunder' in obtaining Mr. Morgan's confessional statement," said the judge, obviously also confused.

"Correct, Your Honor. I simply wanted to put in play the fact that—because the crime my client may have committed has obviously been construed by the District Attorney as part-and-parcel of the RICO charge of a organized criminal enterprise run by Mr. Durwood—your prior application of the prophylactic Exclusionary Rule to protect Mr. Durwood from being infected by evidence obtained by my client must also be, uh, 'put on' to make such evidence inadmissible against Mr. Morgan."

Prophylactic?

"Apples-and-oranges!" said Fisher—the out-of-town lawyer's name was Morton P. Fisher — and though Yours Truly had not testified against his client— a legal angler, set on hooking Yours Truly. But…

"You yourself, Counselor, acknowledged that my client's actions are part of a single 'ball of wax'," said Willis. "And indeed,

Mr. Morgan's possibly criminal bungling did in fact play an evidentiary part in the RICO charges that your client engaged in a conspiracy to thwart an investigation of his criminal enterprise."

Ohhh...

"Ridiculous! Morgan was not part of my client's alleged criminal enterprise," said Fisher. "For crying out loud, he was employed by the right-wing SOW vigilantes to incriminate Mr. Durwood."

Ohhh...

"Yeah, just like the incompetent deputy sheriff," the D. A. shouted, "Morgan's bungled investigation of goings on at the Second Circle Club effectively abetted Durante's sabotage of my RICO case!"

Ohhh...

"Again, Your Honor, the District Attorney and... and this... this 'country lawyer are mixing apples-and-oranges in an attempt to confuse the Court!" said Durante's big-city attorney.

Ohhh...

"As observed after-the-fact by Adam, a rotten apple spoils a whole barrel," said his own country lawyer. "Given the Court's prior application of the Exclusionary Rule to not admit evidence against Mr. Durante provided by my 'blundering' client, for Your Honor to now admit into evidence my Mr. Morgan's confessional statement for any purpose—including RICO prosecution of himself in order to prosecute Durante—would be to befoul this courtroom with fruit of a poison tree."

Ohhhhh...

"The fruit, though perhaps somewhat wormy, is entirely edible, Your Honor!" Morton P. Fisher contended, but...

"Apples-to-apples," said his country lawyer, "to deter unconstitutional acts committed 'under color of law' a correct application of the Exclusionary Rule in this case doubly requires that Max Morgan—both wrongdoer and bungler—go free!"

Ohhhhh...

Max, still in the witness box, detected—or maybe just hopefully imagined—a slight cooling of the hot seat, and...

Judge Dwight scratched his jaw. Looking more confused, His Honor put down the gavel... hmmmed... then said: "The argument made by Counsel for Mr. Morgan seems to be, in effect, that by virtue of his client's bungling of his unvirtuous investigation of Mr. Durante's activities—in violation of his own constitutional right to, say, be free to pursue happiness—makes him both bungling constable and victim deserving of disregard of evidence against him under the Exclusionary Rule."

"Correct, You Honor. The law..."

"The law, as famously observed by Charles Dickens," said Judge Dwight, "is sometimes an ass."

Ohhhhh...

"A pithy observation indeed, Your Honor," said Willis V. Willis. "However, as a simple country lawyer, I would respectfully add—in the approximate words of the great Oriental philosopher, Bruce Lee—the error of riding an ass to search for an ass is compounded into two wrongs by failure to dismount."

Ohhhhh...

As the old judge again raised the gavel, Max braced himself to face music, possibly the old country-and-western tune: *He's In the Jailhouse Now.*

"Hmmm," Judge Dwight again hmmmed, with fishy eyes aimed at both the D. A. and Durndest Durwood's lawyer from Oklahoma City. "Okay, you two, out of here!" His Honor then declared. "RICO charges against Mr. Morgan for blundered burgling are hereby dismissed, with prejudice."

Bang!

THE
END

DEAD MAN'S HAND

A Maximo Morgan Mystery

AUGUST

WILLIAM LEROY

AUGUST

DEAD MAN'S HAND

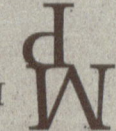

Mossik Press

ISBN 979-8-9869494-8-2
$7.99

TUESDAY

August 5, 2025

CHAPTER ONE

Max twittered his thumbs.

It was the dangerous season: the hot, sultry dog-eat-dog days of August when crime rates in general and the homicide rate in particular were usually at their highest levels. In and around his hometown turf of Henryetta, Oklahoma, however, no such luck.

Yeah, though irritability and suspicion hung in the muggy air like bad body odor, complaints of wrongdoing recently put on his plate had been limited to beefs about increased fees for the Notary Public stamping services he provided to Mister Quickie copy shop customers in lieu of paying rent, along with more than usual bitching about the poor quality of snacks served by the vending machine Quickie had installed in the workstation cubicle that served as his office. Still, there was always hope. According to the radio weatherman, today in particular would be the kind of day that often led to mischief, and...

Hello, into the cubicle came an old codger... dang it, with sheets of paper in hand. Max reached for his Notary stamper, but...

"Are you the private detective known as the Fat Man?" said the codger, taking a seat in the client chair.

"Maximo Morgan's the name, private dicking's my game. And yeah, Yours Truly walks in the gumshoe footsteps of Brad Runyon a/k/a the original Fat Man back in the days and nights of *Noir*. What kind of mischief is afoot, Mr....?"

"Lyon, Robert Lyon, but everyone has always called me 'Tots', short for *totchli*, the ancient Mexican word for 'rabbit'. My parents were, uh, strange. But otherwise, no mischief. Far from

it…"

"Too bad. If you had a hot-to-trot Missus who skipped town with another dog in heat, or if some mutt with a bone to pick was stalking you…"

"I just got off a bus from Hollywood with a movie deal," the walk-in said, putting the sheets of paper on the desk. "And you, Maximo Morgan, are in on it."

Max's ears perked up.

Lyon explained that a couple of weeks ago he'd got off a westbound bus for a local pit stop, and in a men's room had come across a typed manuscript. Back on the bus, he had started reading and—when he woke up in LaLa Land—realized he had stumbled onto the makings of a blockbuster movie…

Max sat up straighter.

… right in the wheelhouse of longtime friends who were bigtime Hollywood moguls.

"In case you don't remember the details, the manuscript goes like this," said the Tinseltown tout, before picking up the sheets of paper and reading aloud:

"'Max sat at his desk inside a Mister Quickie copy shop workstation cubicle that served as his office, twiddling his thumbs. Etcetera, Etcetera, Etcetera. A good-looking dame ankled in… took a seat in the client chair… identified herself as Ms. Beatrice McGregor… and batted her baby blues. In English, but with a funky accent, the dame said she had blown into town from Australia after getting word that her uncle had kicked a bucket and that she was heiress to a nearby family farm. So the lucky lady had looked to be in clover, but…

"'Not clover, just weeds,' the heiress continued. 'But it's my property, being squatted on by distant cousins, and going to seed. Following an encounter with them, I later returned to the local Fountainblue Motel and… This had been dropped off for me,' the skirt said, handing him'—that would be you, Maximo—'a childlike greeting card with a message written on it in block letters. You read: *BEWeaR uv THe BeeST*.'"

Yeah, Max now recalled the lay. Local fuzz had brushed off

what looked to be a run-of-the-mill family dust-up. And Yours Truly had also suspected the dame's cousins out at that weedy farm had likely dropped off the unwelcoming message. But with time on his hands, he had taken the immigrant damsel in distress under a wing. And the teenaged kid who jotted case reports for him—like Doc Watson did for Sherlock Holmes and Mickey Spillane did for Mike Hammer—must have mislaid the beginning of a "manuscript" documenting *Case of Dogs in a Manger*.

"'After breakfast the next day, Yours Truly ankled along Main Street to the Fountainblue Motel, spotted cops on the premises, and…'"

"No need to go into the gory details," Max now said, recalling the scene he'd ankled into: A white blouse the client had been wearing the day before—soaked in blood—lying in the alley behind the motel.

"The 'case report' then goes on and on about your background," said Lyon, rifling through the noticeably not dog-eared stack of pages. "Devouring your deceased father's attic cache of pulp detective novels when you were a teenager… Countless hours spent with your mother, watching tv and re-working cases of *Murder, She Wrote* during and after your twenty-five-year career with the U.S. Postal Service… Discovery of cd recordings of the oldtime radio accounts of the private dickwork of Brad Runyon a/k/a the Fat Man. Overweight, but light on his feet, and a good dancer. Hardboiled, but refined, and a natty dresser. A bulldog when pursuing leads in cases of possible murrrderrr."

The teenaged case report jotter was a wannabe private dick, a protege of sorts, who listened-and-learned at the gumshoed feet, so to speak, of Yours Truly. Eager as a new bride, but inclined to carelessness.

"Then, nothing," said the Hollywood scout in his own words. "This copy of the manuscript trails off with you looking down at the evidence of what appeared to be a vicious assault on your client and complaining that stray dogs had been allowed to contaminate the possible crime scene. What happened next?"

"Local flatfoots took over the investigation," Max explained. "Clueless Barney Fifes detected only that a jailbird had escaped from the county's Iron Bars Hotel in Okmulgee days before. But a pack of bloodhounds failed to pick up the con's odor, and no client remains were found. Case closed."

"Case closed? Criminy, Maximo, I spent my last dime on a bus ticket to get back here for the rest of a story with perhaps an improbably positive outcome in which protagonists were rewarded, antagonists punished, and positive sentiments—preferably love—prevailed. In other words, a story with a Hollywood ending!"

Hard cheese for the Mexican rabbit, not to mention for Yours Truly. But in the local gumshoe game that's how the cheddar sometimes crumbled. More often than not actually, Max silently noted with a sigh. Yeah, like a lot of his lays, *Case of Dogs in a Manger* had come to a more probable than not Henryetta, Oklahoma ending.

CHAPTER TWO

Arf! Arf! Arf! Arooooo…

Inside a mobile home parked on a farm in the hill-and-holler area northwest of town, Larry "Bear" McGregor opened an eye.

Arf! Arf! Arf! Arooooo…

He sniffed the air.

Arf! Arf! Arf! Arooooo…

Dang it, not only had the wife, "Foxy", woke him up by bringing her pack of Beagle hounds from their kennel to right out front of the house…

Arf! Arf! Arf! Arooooo…

… now she was feeding her "darlings" *Stella & Chewy* dried rabbit patties that cost more than t-bone steaks.

As he had tried to explain to his late pa, dislike of early rising was one of the reasons he was not cut out to be a farmer. Fine, the old man had huffed, before threatening to leave the family homestead to a niece living distantly, even though he—the old man's son and heir—had took to raising a patch of weed in a far north corner of the property. And sure enough, soon as Pa died in the fire that burned down the big house, a Cousin Beatrice had showed up, claiming she had a right to have the whole eighty acres.

Arf! Arf! Arf! Arooooo…

But the ornery cousin's interest in the farm didn't last long. And though he himself had decided that—in addition to dislike of early rising and hard work—he was not cut out for growing marijuana as a profitable occupation, he had stuck to it, while the wife—calling herself "Mistress of Henryetta Hounds"—wasted

her time…

Arf! Arf! Arf! Arooooo…

Bear closed his eye and tried to catch a few more winks, but… Dog-gone-it, now into her forties, Foxy had no younguns to look after, and no other relations—except a no-account brother that she doted on whenever he was around—but took better care of those Beagle dogs than she had ever took care of him, her mate since high school.

The wife had read a lot of books about Beagles, and was all the time ruining their tv time together by telling about such things as how her dog called "Babbler"—a "gyp" a/k/a bitch—"though somewhat inclined to open early with tongue, threw the most musical drawn out notes so inspiring to the others"… about how the one called "Driver" was "a fast runner a/k/a flier, but also a well trained anchor hound, good at holding other hunters at check points for picking up changes in directions of scent" and…

Blah, Blah, Blah: "Bouncer" was a jumper, good at catching sight of the zigging-and-zagging of rabbits when chasing… "Picker", another gyp, older than the others but with a specially "wet nose", supposedly followed trails slowly, "methodically, and wisely"… The one called "Snoopy", on the other hand, needed watching—and sometimes "rating by whip or word"—the "Mistress of Hounds" was all the time saying about a little runt, not only because he was still young, but also because he had been sired by…

Arf! Arf! Arf! Arooooo…

Both eyes popped open, a chill ran down Bear's spine. Snoopy's pa was the wife's ex so-called brag-dog, supposedly perfect in "confirmation" and a dogged hunter, but… Dang it, that hound from hell called "Killer" had ruined their happy home life.

Arf! Arf! Arf! Arooooo…

Everyone who crossed paths with the beast feared its nasty attitude, with darn good reason, and the sumbitch had disliked him in particular at first sight. The wife's brag-dog might have been high-classed, and he did catch a lot of rabbits, but finally, about two months ago even Foxy had been horrified—not by

her favorite dog's vicious habit of slaughtering little bunnies by the dozens—but by his attacks on her other hounds, including Snoopy.

Thankfully, the bloodthirsty Beagle had been sent away, hopefully to a restaurant kitchen in China where, people said, Communists ate dogs. But…

Arf! Arf! Arf! Arooooo… Arf! Arf! Arf! Arooooo… Arf! Arf! Arf!…

What the heck?! Into the mobile home came the pack of barking, braying, howling dogs…

Arooooo… Aroooo… Arooooo…

… followed by the wife, cracking a whip!

"Hoick! Hoick! Hoick!" she shouted to cheer on the home invasion.

Arooooo… Arooooo…

"Down! Down, my darlings," the Mistress then shouted at the dogs.

"Up! Up! you lazy sumbitch!" the Missus more sternly shouted at him.

Arooooo…

Foxy claimed that after a morning workout to train for a big Okmulgee County Beagle Hunt in October, it was now too hot for her pets to be put in the kennel, and she didn't want him—supposedly master of the house—interrupting their naps.

"Out! Out! Out!"

But… But… But, he'd not yet had breakfast, Bear protested, while picking up shoes, pants and a shirt.

Out on the front stoop, the wife scooped a serving of cheap *Victor Edge Energy* chow into a bowl and ordered him to have a picnic breakfast when he got to work.

Halfway up a hill on the way to his weed patch, Bear looked back and… Aha! Foxy was all the time going across the south forty to a neighboring farm—where a woman who raised racing pigeons had set up a beauty parlor inside her house—but always came back with her frizzy red hair not even combed. And now she was carrying two bowls of dried rabbit patties in that direction.

Ha! Like the wife was all the time telling him, he might be "dumber than the average bear", but he wasn't as stupid as she and about everyone else thought. With his own wet nose he had picked up a smell, and knew the beautician had left her husband, Gary Lee "Big Bert" Haggard, a sumbitch as mean and feared as the heartless hound from Hell named Killer.

CHAPTER THREE

After taking Tots Lyon home to the small frame house he had lived in with his mom since birth, Max assigned a twin bed to his new best friend, who was out of cash and in need of a place to lay his head. At ends of the days ahead—now that the Hollywood expert had convinced him to re-open *Case of Dogs in a Manger*—bunking together in his bedroom would allow them to lay their heads together and compare notes from their joint investigation into the suspicious disappearance of his client, Beatrice McGregor.

Mom had furnished the room with an extra bed during his childhood, hoping he would someday host sleep-overs with friends, and had warmly welcomed Tots to stay as long as he wanted. But now, back in the kitchen for lunch...

"I don't see why your associates out in Hollywood would want to make a movie of a true story that starts with practically nothing happening, and has no ending of any kind in sight," she said to their guest. "As far as anyone knows, that escaped jailbird had nothing to do with the 'disappearance' of that woman, or even that she met with foul play. Lots of Max's 'clients' never come back after first meetings."

"Lots of famous narratives were once incomplete due to, say, untimely authors' deaths," said Tots. "Take for instance, *The Mystery of Edwin Drood*, started by Charles Dickens but stalled at the point when Drood's torn coat was found on a river bank after he went missing. Various others took cracks at doping out who likely did in Drood. Heck, someone even produced a Broadway musical in which a private detective named Dick

Datchery appeared on the scene and sang:

♫I come to town/ My ear at every door/ Half the clown, yet crafty to the core… ♫

"Well yes, but why not use an already completed case report jotted by the teenaged kid, Max's so-called 'Watson'. For instance, the *Case of* … "

♫A kettle of fish, I'll fry/ I'll hook each goose to mix a metaphor♫

"Well yes, but in *Case of a Suspected…*"

"I myself saw two performances of *Drood*, and even though warned at the end of Act I— ♫Don't fall back on your assumptions/ Hasty presumptions might do you in♫— both times pegged a wrong suspect as Edwin Drood's likely killer."

"Well, yes, but in *Case of a Suspected Teenaged Two-Timer*, Max stumbled into solving an actual murder."

"I'm just a networker," Tots continued. "Stanley Stanley is the creative partner at the Stanley & Stanley Studio," said the Hollywood networker, who had grown up with Stanley and Stanford Stanley in Oklahoma City. "And Stanley has wanted to make a movie with an inheritance angle and Hollywood ending since childhood."

"Oh, something along the lines of *Case of Knives Out*? Max and I were appalled by those greedy relatives of that poor man, dying of cancer, who cut his own throat and left his fortune to a nurse who had cared for him."

Yes and no, according to Tots. While the Stanley & Stanley business guy, Stanford Stanley, was keen on the potential murder angle of *Case of Dogs in a Manger*, Stanley Stanley had been both inspired and frustrated during his youth by a Looney Tunes flick titled *The Wabbit Who Came to Supper*, in which a pesky rabbit—chased to ground by dogs for a shotgun toting hunter named Fudd—was saved when a mailman delivered to the hunter a letter from an Uncle Louie, promising to leave the nephew three million dollars on condition that he never harm animals, especially rabbits. As a result…

Buzz. Buzz. Buzz.

"Stan, my man," said Tots into his phone. "Stan, my other man," the Hollywood networker then said in what must have been a conference call.

"Oh yeah, dotting i's and crossing t's with our man, Maxie, as we speak."

"Uh huh…

"Uh huh…

"Got it: Not too tight-assed…

"Uh huh…

"Think outside the box. Got it.

"Uh huh…

"Uh huh…

"Wheels in motion. No *problemo.*

"*Ciao.*

"*Ciao.*"

Max had always wondered what networkers did for a living, and now understood that…

"Both Stans are excited about *Case of The Woman Who Came to Supper* but want to make sure that we…"

Case of The Woman Who Came to Supper?

"Just a working title for now, Max. To make movies you gotta start loosey-goosey and allow for artistic license."

"Artistic license for a true-crime case report?"

"<u>Based</u> on a real-life case report, Max. We may have to, uh, speculate about details such as, say, why an old Oklahoma farmer would leave local acreage to a, quote, 'niece' supposedly living in Australia. And whether the 'heiress' is going to end up dead or alive."

"But… But… But… If the dame didn't buy the farm, it won't be a murrrderrr mystery."

"Worked onstage in *Drood,*" said Tots. "In six-hundred and eight standing-room-only Broadway performances, Edwin Drood showed up at the end, alive and well. Said he had faked his death in order to see how his enemies would react."

"Almost just like in *Case of Knives Out!*" Mom exclaimed. "The dying man who wanted to spite his greedy relatives—not

knowing that his nurse was prone to vomiting when telling a lie—told her to create a false alibi to cover up her involvement in his suicide."

Hmmm.

Max wondered how his involvement in 'artistic license' might affect his P.I. license and…

Hmmm.

… also wondered if he himself would toss cookies if required to diddle facts of a case for Hollywood fame and fortune.

♫Don't fall back on your assumptions ♫ Tots again semi-sang. ♫Hasty presumptions might do you in♫

CHAPTER FOUR

At the wheel of the Morgan family's brown Buick sedan, aha, on the side of the rutted dirt road up ahead, Tots spotted a leaning post topped by a mailbox. Slowed to a crawl, he detected vestiges of the name *McGregor* painted on the rusted metal box. He stopped, cut the engine, and got out of the car.

While Max remained in town to re-investigate circumstances surrounding the disappearance and presumed demise of the heiress, Beatrice McGregor, his own "routine assignment" was to interview the possibly murderous cousins presumably residing on the farm at the center of a disputed inheritance scenario, but...

Walking up a weedy driveway, Tots began to have doubts about the movie potential of *Case of The Woman Who Came to Supper*. The hilly terrain consisted mainly of outcrops of rock. Except for scrub brush, the ground was devoid of vegetation, and the air seemingly unpopulated by birds, but...

Arooooo...

Despite the midday August heat, the distant sound of a howling coyote, or perhaps even a wolf, made shivers run up and down his back and...

Arooooo...

... at the end of the driveway, he saw only a dilapidated trailer house set on cinder blocks.

Arooooo...

Stepping onto a stoop at the mobile home's front door, raising a fist to knock...

Arf! Arf! Arf! Arooooo...

Tots stumbled backward off the stoop.

Arf! Arf! Arf! Arooooo…
OMG! The trailer was a mobile doghouse!
Arf! Arf! Arf! Arooooo…
Hightailing back toward the parked car…
Buzz. Buzz. Buzz.
Tots stopped in his tracks and…
"Stan, my man," he said into his phone.
"Stan, my other man," he then said.
"Uh huh.
"Uh huh.
"Checking out the inherited, uh, estate as we speak."
They would have no trouble casting dogs to chase a "wabbit" for on-location filming, he reported. But as for a setting befitting the ancestral home of a rich "Uncle Louie" such as would spark a fight over inheritance…
"Uh huh.
"Uh huh.
"Okay, but… "
Though only a networker, Tots ventured to suggest to the two Hollywood moguls that they might want to re-think outside the box about casting Clooney in the role of the local private detective.But…
"Uh huh.
"Uh huh."
Told that business arrangements of pre-production were too far along to make changes—and that he should stick to nailing down the picture's storyline—Tots got back into the Buick and… After driving slowly southward on the rutted dirt road for a short distance… aha, spotted a mailbox posted at the entrance to a driveway hopefully leading to the main house of a gentleman's farm suitable for perhaps fox hunting. And, aha, a somewhat rusted metal sign…

La Maison Derriere Loft
Breeding & Hair Done by Appointment Only

… identified entrance to possibly a gentleman's horse farm.
Walking up a driveway, uh oh, another sign warned BEWARE

THE BIRD… and set against one of a cluster of buildings was a row of what looked to be pigeon coops.

On a somewhat rickety front porch of a somewhat overly "shabby chic" house, he knocked on a somewhat sagging screen door and…

"Whatta you want?" said a towering figure — standing in the opened doorway with a large bird perched on his shoulder — instantly bringing to Tots' mind the terrifying image of a notorious bully from his teenaged years: "Big Mo" Molenovsky!

"Uh… Uh… Uh, just looking for the McGregor farm," he managed to answer.

"Do I look like a dumber-than-dirt drug dealing faggot?"

"No, no, not at all. Sorry, I must have made a wrong turn."

"You a private dick, sent by the ex-wife to rescue her racing birds?"

"No, no, I'm not a dick. I'm just a Hollywood networker."

"Yeah, sure. Tell that bitch Donald must've got 'em," the "Big Mo" said with a smirk, accompanied by a nod toward his feathered companion that — OMG! — looked to be an f'ing falcon, tethered, thankfully, by a chain latched to a clawed foot. "All dead, along with every damn pigeon and other pest caught roaming hereabouts, except, so far, that other bitch's dogs."

With the inner door thankfully slammed in his face, Tots — drenched in sweat — hopped off the rickety porch and hightailed back down the driveway, soaked in relief to have been a pest spared, so far, by a "Big Mo" and the bird of prey named Donald.

CHAPTER FIVE

Max exited the local police station and ankled along Main Street toward the next stop in his re-investigation into the re-opened and re-named *Case of The Woman Who Came to Supper*.

At the police station, however, a dame on desk duty informed him that the town's uniformed Barney Fifes, along with the chief—a clueless do-nutter named Potter—were out on patrol, but… looked into a file cabinet and confirmed that, yeah, on July 10th the McGregor broad had filed a complaint.

The clerk personally recalled that the woman from overseas had waved what she claimed to be a will entitling her to possession of a nearby farm—demanding that the fuzz forcibly evict cousins from the property—but refused to allow a full reading of the document supposedly conveying legal title to her until she had hired a lawyer.

Hmmm.

Vaguely recalling that he himself had not bothered to eyeball a last will and testament backing the client's claim—and not recalling that Yours Truly had ever notarized such of document for any nearby county resident named John McGregor—Max worried that lack of a legit inheritance angle might queer the pending movie deal.

According to Tochtli Lyon, the creative Stan out in LaLa Land had been "troubled" since childhood by how *The Wabbit Who Came to Supper* flick turned out. After putting up with a pesky rabbit in order to meet a will's conditions for a three million dollar windfall, Fudd, the inheritor of the fortune, got notice that after taxes he not only netted nothing, but owed two

bucks out of his own pocket to Uncle Sam. And reportedly since then the creative Stan had been obsessed with finding a similar semi-true case with a happy Hollywood ending.

Dang it, lays of *noir* type—such as *Percy Wilson's Case of Where There's a Will There's a Weigh*—were Yours Truly's bag. In that Wilson whodunnit a wealthy yachtsman, missing at sea and declared dead, had left his fortune to a slightly overweight second wife on condition that she—for her own sake—lose one hundred pounds in one hundred days. Sure enough, the widow died of malnutrition and the yachtsman washed ashore, alive and well, in a dinghy also occupied by a bosomy babe sporting an engagement ring. Not exactly a Hollywood ending, and never made into a movie, but...

With a sigh, Max arrived at the Fountainblue Motel, where his own missing client was last seen, hours before her bloody blouse was found in an adjacent alley.

He'd had a couple of prior run-ins with the motel proprietor, an odd duck named Hugo Lice. Most recently in connection with *Case of One Shoe Blues,* in which a local gathering of suspected international criminals had turned out to be a group of famous women's shoe designers and... Yeah, now he spotted the baldy, seated behind the check-in counter, watching tv.

"Sorry to interrupt the soap opera, Lice. Looking into the disappearance of the broad who lost her shirt on the premises about a month ago. Ms. Beatrice McGregor by name."

Now wise to not messing with Yours Truly, the motel owner got up from the boob tube, came to the counter, and opened a ledger. After thumbing through only a few pages...

"Yes, here she is. Checked in on July 6th."

"Hmmm," Max hmmmed. The missing client didn't complain to police until four days later.

"*MasterCard* refused to honor the room charge due to questions about..."

"Yeah, questions about the dame's disappearance and likely murrrderrr are what I'm looking into, Lice. This joint happen to have a safe deposit box for any of the guest's valuables that might

have been deposited?"

"Yes, but I've already…"

"Let's have a look."

Lice swiveled, took a pink shoe box labeled *Gucci* off a shelf and put it on the counter. Inside the box… an old wristwatch … a Roscoe and two or three spare bullets… a partial denture… and bingo: a folded set of documents wrapped in a rubber band that… dang it, turned out to be not a last will and testament of an Uncle McGregor… only a marriage license application and pre-nup agreement, both signed by only a joker named "Todd Reynard".

Hmmm.

Based on information picked up in *Case of One Shoe Blues,* Max dismissed possibility that the client—like the hunted victim in Brad Runyon's *Case of the Crooked Horse*—might have hidden the will under loosened wallpaper in her room. In a vain attempt to upgrade the flea bag, Lice had installed knotty pine paneling and…

"What went wrong, Hugo, did the McGregor broad catch you peeping through another knot hole?"

"That hole was drilled by a guest to spy on another guest, and has long been plugged!"

"Okay, don't get your boxers in a bunch. How about lost-and-found?"

As the innkeeper went into a back room, Max wondered if his client had been on the level.

For instance, did Beatrice McGregor go willingly into the alley in dark of night, and if so, why? Without a shred of evidence, cops had speculated that the motel guest had ducked out for a smoke, but more to the point…

As Lice returned to the counter with a bushel-size cardboard box in his arms, Max wondered why the McGregor broad had refused to allow cops to read her uncle's will.

Inside the lost-and-found box, he detected an argyle sock… a tooth brush… a pair of men's boxers… a pair of men's pants… a jacket… a cylindrical vibrating gadget… No women's items,

but… hello, at the bottom of the box… a dame's shoe… red… missing its high-heel.

Hmmm.

Ms. McGregor had hobbled to the motel check-in counter wearing the "ruined peek-a-boo pump", Lice claimed to now recall. Must have lost the other one while out and about, the suspiciously leering motelier suggested, while fondling the evidence.

Or found this one, Max himself speculated after also sniffing the footwear.

Either way—one shoe off or one shoe on—something foul was afoot in *Case of The Woman Who Came to Supper*.

CHAPTER SIX

♫**I'm the fastest bird of prey/ Bird of prey, bird of prey...** ♫

As an annoying kindergarten song kept on blasting from pole-mounted loudspeakers, Bear McGregor stood at an edge of his weed patch, urinating. Rabbits were supposedly put off by loud noise and the aroma of predator pee. And by the odor of marigolds, geraniums, onions, coffee grounds and shreds of *Irish Spring* soap. In addition to wire fencing around the patch, he'd tried all the old wives' remedies, except for the dangerous one his own old wife had offered.

♫**I find the highest perch to roost/ Perch to roost, perch to roost...** ♫

Along with bears, foxes, wolves, coyotes, cats, raccoons, possums, weasels, falcons and humans, dogs were natural enemies of rabbits, and the wife's whole reason for having a pack of Beagles was to hunt the also long-eared rascals. But Foxy ordinarily kept her little darlings in a kennel from dusk-to-dawn when cottontails were mainly out and about. And when hunting, the Mistress of Hounds usually cracked a whip to keep the mutts on the scent of only one or two rabbits at a time. Dang it, a single buck and two does could produce fifty bunnies a year!

♫**I make a steep drop at great speed/ Two hundred miles-an-hour at least, at least...** ♫

Unlike his not so dearly departed pa, Bear had never hated rabbits, not even when his ma died of rabbit fever. At age ten, he'd felt 'specially bad for keeping a cuddly all-white pet Hotot named Harvey that Ma had given to him at Easter. And... He now shuddered to recall the old man lecturing how important it

was for him to keep-up his strength, and… and… and only after dinner, announcing that Harvey had been "tasty".

For years afterward he had been forced to join in watching an old movie called *Watership Down*, counting out loud the mostly bloody deaths of sixty-three long-eared "killers". Just a few weeks ago, his pa—waving a rake and shouting that he would have rabbit pies for supper after catching him in the act of leaving carrots around the weed patch—had took a hand to him and refused to believe that he'd only intended to bribe the killers to not nibble his cannabis crop.

♫**My talons and beak are fierce/ They can surely, surely pierce, surely pierce…** ♫

Bear zipped-up his pants and waded into the weed… Down on hands-and-knees, he lumbered between rows of plants… Overnight damage looked to be minimal. Big Bert Haggard's "protection plan" looked to be working, though a part of him hated to admit anything to the sumbitch's credit. Since moving onto the neighboring farm, Haggard danger had hung above the whole weed patch and beyond like a threatening… Well, according to Foxy, Big Bert's ex-wife had told that he got the idea of naming his trained bird of prey after the pet of a character in old *Saturday Night Live* re-runs called…

Dang it, he hisself was just as big as the big bully, probably stronger, and in a fair fight between just the two of them would knock the unfriendly neighbor's head clean off, but…

♫**I'm the fastest bird of prey/ Bird of prey, bird of prey…** ♫

As if staged in a horror movie, a shadow came over Bear and…

♫**I'm a falcon/ I screech and scream, screech and scream…** ♫

"Whatcha doin' down there, 'Br'er Bear', 'fertilizing' your weeds? Too bad there's no woods around here for you to crap in."

With Big Bert hovering above, which was threatening enough, Bear didn't dare look up to see if the bully's companion, "Donald", was perched on his shoulder. Only due to duress, he'd agreed to pay for the vicious rabbit-hunter's protection of his crop. And though the ferocious falcon bird had killed only a few

invaders during dawn-and-dusk attacks, its low-level swooping, screaming, screeching flights had seemed to pay-off during the past two months. So now...

"Time to pay the piper, McGregor," said the loan shark, who had also installed the audio "scarecrow" system and lent money to buy plants for the current crop of weed. "Past time, in fact, and you know what that means."

Yeah, he wasn't as dumb as everyone thought. Bear now knew that Haggard's plan all along was to get his talons on the farm by way of foreclosure. He himself would not care about losing the McGregor family homestead and moving into town, but Foxy...

"I might've cut you some more slack if your ornery old man had not tried to hand off your inheritance to that bitch from Australia," said his tormentor.

Stifling an urge to eat more humble pie and beg for more time to pay back what he owed, Bear kept his head down and stayed quiet.

"I'll be out hunting with Donald on my own place tomorrow, Br'er Bear. So it'll be after dark when I come by to settle things, and to personally tell Foxy she can stay in the mobile house, under certain conditions."

Enraged by suspicion that the sumbitch had already got the wife in his beak, Bear slowly counted to ten... then summoned enough courage to raise his head... to look upward... and seeing Big Bert gone but the Donald now soaring above him... to at least try to stare down the sharp-eyed bird of prey... with a growl and blast of bad odor.

CHAPTER SEVEN

During Max's Max's account of his day's dickwork at the police station and Fountainblue Motel, Tots—only nibbling at only a salad—had not perked up his ears. And now, instead of reporting results his own assignment to look into goings-on out at the McGregor farm, his so-called co-investigator remained mum as an oyster.

So after Mom got up from the kitchen table and went to watch tv, Yours Truly rolled up his sleeves, so to speak, and started shucking, again so to speak.

Opening up like a... like a shucked oyster, the obviously nervous networker whined that the farm at the center of the inheritance angle to *Case of The Woman Who Came to Supper* was nowhere near worth three million bucks... that no one in his or her right mind would care about getting or losing the property by way of an old man's will or otherwise... and that the Stanleys would no doubt dump the movie project if Yours Truly didn't come up with an angle that had potential for a Hollywood ending.

In other words, Lyon—though desperate to make a buck and likely too broke to get out of Dodge—was a softboiled amateur, likely to be of no help in cracking the case of Beatrice McGregor's suspicious disappearance. And the creative Stan in charge of making a movie documenting the case sounded like also a wuss. In other other word, Yours Truly...

Knock. Knock. Knock.

Max got up from the table, went to the front door, opened it and... Standing there was the teenaged kid—his "Watson"—who

had jotted the first few pages of the case report for *Case of Dogs in a Manger.*

"Sorry to barge in after hours, Mr. Max," he said, "but I was riding by on my bike, and wondered if anything was up that needed jotting down."

Max made introductions and—after the kid took Mom's vacated chair at the table—put the young case report jotter wise to his current lay.

"But... But... But I am your Doc Watson, and your Mickey Spillane," the unsavvy teenager sputtered. "I came up with the idea of jotting your case reports, Mr. Max. It's not fair for you to hand the *Case of Dogs in a Manger* to Hollywood hacks."

"Get over it, kid. Heck, based on Spillane's notes, a jotter named Max Allan Collins took over Mike Hammer's case reporting, and has produced dozens of bestsellers."

"Yeah, but only because Mr. Spillane bought the farm," the kid argued. "You're selling out, Mr. Max, you're putting your reputation and self respect at risk for a shot at Hollywood fame and fortune."

Contending that Tinseltown had a sordid history of butchering real crime case reports, the kid reminded him that Yours Truly himself had bitterly complained about how movie moguls had made a hash out of Mike Hammer's *Case of I, The Jury,* twice. For a 1982 documentary, they just ripped off the title of the bestseller and got studio scribblers to make up a story involving the C.I.A. that wasn't even set in the *Noir.* Even worse, in a 1952 Hollywood version...

"For crying out loud, Mr. Max, you know Mr. Spillane's account of the case ending by heart," said the kid. "Charlotte Manning came onto Hammer like a cherry tart on a pastry trolley. Her thumbs hooked the fragile silk of her panties and pulled them down. She stepped out of them as delicately as one coming from a bathtub. The blonde knockout leaned over to kiss Mike, her arms held out to embrace him, and..."

Yeah, as garishly illustrated on the lurid cover of the pulp report that had inspired Yours Truly to someday become a

private dick, those arms were really reaching for a gat stashed in a potted plant. Mike, waiting to be kissed, was really set up to have his head blown off when the roar of his own Roscoe shook the room. The *femme fatale* staggered back a step. A thin trickle of blood welled out of her naked belly. "How could you?" she asked, to which Mike answered...

"In the Hollywood version of events, Charlotte Manning is shown taking off a raincoat, a scarf, her shoes, and that's it!" the het-up kid continued. "She isn't naked when Mike plugs her, and that's not even the ending. On film, the hardboiled private dick supposedly doesn't say "It was easy", and leave it at that. On the big screen, he supposedly calls for a casket, and says, yeah, his cop buddy—Pat Chambers—would get the killer the fuzz were after, but—with a sob—that he himself would have only memories of the broad."

"That's the kind of tweak that adds a sentimental touch typical of occasionally unhappy Hollywood endings," Tots opined, but the kid...

"What the heck, Mr. Dashiell Hammett jotted case reports for not only Brad Runyon a/k/a the original Fat Man, but also for Mr. Nick Charles a/k/a the Thin Man, and must have been sick to his stomach about the *Song of the Thin Man* movie that made the lay look like a nightclub act featuring a torch song singer, who... "

"Songs help move murder mysteries along," said Tots, "by hinting at hidden storylines and dropping clues."

"In the Thin Man case, storylines 'hinted at' by the song, *Oh Where, Oh Where Has My Little Dog Gone* must have stayed hidden," said the young jotter, who had also studied most if not all the recorded cases handled by famous gumshoes back in the *Noir*.

"Nick Charles and his wife Nora had a little dog named Asta that figured in some of their cases," Tots pointed out, but...

"Like a famous movie mogul admitted, all that Hollywood writers do is change the words," the kid wailed. "For *Case of Dogs in a Manger* they would probably slip in a love story".

"So what?" Tots answered. "Like another famous movie mogul said, 'There's only sure-fire storyline: Boy meets girl. Boy loses girl. Boy gets girl back.'"

"Heck, Mr. Max, the reason you hired, uh, engaged me to write up your cases was to make sure your lays would be accurately put on the record," the kid reminded him. "If not for Dr. Watson, no one would have heard of Sherlock Holmes."

"Hey, maybe the Stans would agree to giving you a writing credit on the big screen," said Tots to the kid; and to Yours Truly: "Maybe they would even think outside the box and put you in the role of 'Maximo Morgan, the Fat Man'."

Bingo!

With that settled to everyone's satisfaction, Max reached into a brown paper sack and retrieved the lost-and-found or found-and-lost woman's shoe that he'd detected while grilling the Fountainblue Motel proprietor, Hugo Lice.

"Yeah, Stanley Stanley might go for a *Cinderella* angle," said Tots with renewed pep. "You know, maybe Miss McGregor lost the shoe after balling with a 'prince' at the motel and ends up a 'princess'."

"More realistically," said the kid, "Peter Rabbit lost both shoes during a raid on an old man's garden after his father got caught stealing carrots and ended up in a pie!"

"Stanley Stanley would never go for a dark Orson-Wellian angle," said Tots, "but Stanford Stanley..."

"More likely the Australian heiress lost the footwear while fleeing from rival inheritors out at that farm," the kid continued, and... "Hmmm," the bookish jotter hmmed, with a thoughtful hand to his chin.

Max had a hunch the McGregor skirt had found the heel-less "peek-a-boo pump" out at that farm. Or the client might have wrestled it off the foot of one of her cousins — likely a broad — in a scuffle.

"As I recall from your original investigation, Mr. Maximo, you said you detected paw prints at the scene of the bloody blouse. Bring to mind the famous Sherlock Holmes case?"

On yeah, the so-called "curious case" of the dog that didn't bark. Totally irrelevant.

"No, that was in Case of Silver Blaze," said the kid, who then went on to also "remind" him that in Holmes' Case of The Hound of the Baskervilles, the British detective's client—a Sir Charles Baskerville, also blown into town from Australia—had also checked into a hotel... also intent on making a claim to inheritance of a family estate... also received a message warning him: "As you value your life, or your reason, keep away from the moor." And later realized that a single boot had gone missing from his luggage.

Yeah, hotel and motel staffs were known to have sticky fingers, which was one of the reasons Yours Truly, when traveling, always slept with his duds and footwear on, his wallet under a pillow, and one private eye open.

"Well yeah, better to be safe than sorry, Mr. Max. But in Mr. Holmes' case it turned out that a distant Baskerville cousin—living on a neighboring estate under a false identity—had taken the boot in order to put a vicious hound onto the scent of his rival for the inheritance."

"Neighbor?!" said Tots, rising halfway out of his chair "No, that dog won't hunt, as I'm told they say in these parts. Wandering afield is a sure way to ruin a movie mystery," the Hollywood networker advised, but...

The kid may have stumbled onto an angle, Max admitted silently to himself. Now that Yours Truly thought about it, the note sent to the missing McGregor broad—"Bewear uv The Beest"—sounded like some kind of set-up. And now he recalled that when Totchli Lyon ankled into the Mister Quckie workstation cubicle this morning—with an improbable explanation of how he had got his mitts on the kid's unfinished "manuscript"—the walk-in's exact words were that he had got off a westbound bus to, quote: "see a man about a dog".

Hmmm.

WEDNESDAY

August 6, 2025

CHAPTER EIGHT

Back at the kitchen table with a cuppa morning joe in hand, Max finally reached the last page of Doc Watson's wordy account of *Case of The Hound of the Baskervilles*. Last night the kid's comparison of Sherlock Holmes' famous "adventure" to Yours Truly's current lay had started to make sense. And later, with Lyon whimpering in the other bunk, he himself had tossed and turned while thinking outside a box.

The so-called Hollywood networker had come back from a routine once-over of the McGregor family farm earlier yesterday, obviously nervous as a scared rabbit. At dinner, he'd been mum as a... as an oyster. And when the kid pitched the *Hound of the Baskervilles* angle — pegging a secretly related neighbor of the Baskervilles estate for using a stolen boot to put a vicious dog onto the scent of rival inheritors — Lyon had warned about the storyline wandering "too far afield".

Hmmm.

In a nutshell, Watson's report on the Holmes case was that a distant relative from Australia, living on a next-door estate, exploited a local legend by spraying phosphorescent paint on a vicious dog... scared a current owner of the Baskervilles property to death by heart attack... stole a boot to put the dog onto the scent of a rival heir to the spooky farm... but was mistook for the next intended victim by the hound and was himself fatally mauled.

Yeah, the surly canine "solved" the mystery. Homes, the supposedly brilliant British detective — except to send the legit heir on a fool's errand through a dark and foggy "moor"

as bait—had done practically nothing but skulk around the countryside in foggy *noir*, but was now bragging to his case report jotter about...

Max closed the 169-page Sherlock Holmes book, took a swig of lukewarm java, and mentally compared notes:

In *Case of the Woman Who Came to Supper* the McGregor broad had only "disappeared"... yeah, after making a claim of inheritance but refusing to show a will to local cops... and also claimed to have received a note warning her to beware of a possibly canine "beest"... but may have purposefully ditched the blouse... possibly later bloodied by raccoons fighting over garbage can contents in the motel alley.

And yeah, Yours Truly had later detected nearby paw prints... but possibly if not probably left by stray dogs, not a vicious "hound".

Only the intriguing heel-less shoe—indicating a missing mate—was persuasively in line with evidence doped out by Holmes in *Case of The Hound of the Baskervilles*, but...

"Slept in to allow the sun and Stanley Stanley to rise on the west coast," said Tots, finally finished tossing, turning and possibly plotting. "Got Stan on the phone and, bingo, Max. He likes the *Cinderella* shoe angle as a way to weave a love story into the movie."

Love story?

"I know, I know, Hollywood love is usually not 'hardboiled', but as a famous and successful oldtime movie mogul famously said, 'Let's have some new cliches.'"

"New cliches, yeah. But there's no evidence of romance in the local air."

"I know, I know, but along the lines of what the famous mogul also said about the storyline of one of his pictures, 'Absolutely impossible, but has possibilities.'"

"Way ahead of you," said Max playing his suspicions about the Hollywood networker close to the vest. "Could've been a scam afoot, a wily attempt by the McGregor skirt to pull wool over the private eye of Yours Truly."

"Hmmm," the networker hmmmed. "Now that you mention it, in *The Wabbit Who Came to Supper*, the pesky varmint that the hunter got to be particularly friendly with took advantage and—when booted from the house—faked that he was near death in order to regain sympathy. But after getting the tax bill on his inheritance, Fudd had a hunch he had been scammed. Like I say, what has bothered Stanley Stanley ever since reading part of the kid's unfinished manuscript all the way through is that the storyline was left hanging, without a Hollywood ending."

"Yeah, well, like Yours Truly says: In *Case of The Woman Who Came to Supper*, no way is Maximo Morgan gonna be tricked by a friendly 'rabbit'."

"Well, yes, maybe an attempted fraud was in play at the outset, but Max, picture the McGregor woman as Holly Golightly in *Breakfast at Tiffany's*. She was a bit of a huckster and maybe a hooker, but her neighbor, a writer, fell in love with her and…"

"Speaking of a neighbor…"

"Or if the Audrey Hepburn flick was too far before your time, think of the McGregor woman as Julia Roberts in *Pretty Woman*, who was a hooker but…"

"The McGregor broad isn't, or wasn't a looker, but yeah, possibly a hooker. And Yours Truly 'sees' this case as more likely a 'love story' along the lines of many-a-mystery documented on film back in the *Noir*. Such as *Case of Blonde Crazy*, in which a foxy *femme fatale* teamed up with a bellboy to set up a married hotel guest in a compromising situation and…"

"Okay, okay, in the hands of Stanford Stanley—the unsentimental S&S partner—maybe the storyline takes a dark turn about love versus passing sexual attraction, like in *Fatal Attraction* with Glenn Close, who boiled a pet rabbit, probably alive, and…"

"Maybe," said Max. "But there's no way of knowing exactly what angle the McGregor broad was working—likely in cahoots with some big-city joker—until Yours Truly finds out if the so-called 'heiress' did or did not show a legit last will-and-testament to the 'cousins' out at that farm."

In other words, approximately those of Sherlock Holmes recorded in *Case of The Four*, only after eliminating all which is impossible, whatever remains, however improbable, must be probable.

CHAPTER NINE

"Release the hounds!"

Bear jolted upright in his *Lazy-Boy* recliner—upsetting his bowl of dried rabbit patties but, luckily, not waking any of the wife's dogs napping on the floor around him.

"On Basher! On Slasher!..."

On the mobile home's tv screen, mean old Mr. Burns—owner of the Springfield Nuclear Power Company—was siccing a pack of dogs on a crowd of frightened Christmas carolers.

"On Mangy and Tricksem!"

The bookwormy wife said *Simpsons* re-runs were mostly based on other famous stories, and were "satirical". He hisself had noticed that most of the shows had animals in them. Heck, before the big-house fire he had played and replayed a dvd of *Top Fifty Simpson Bears* that Foxy gave to him for a Christmas.

"On Stalker! On Vicious!..."

Lisa Simpson had a bear picture on the wall above her bed, which was good. On the other hand, a statue in the Springfield town square showed a Jebediah Springfield standing on top of a dead bear that the town founder had killed with his bare hands. And in the *Trash of the Titans* episode Homer put a talking teddy bear named Sir Luv-a-Lot into a garbage can and stomped on the toy.

"On Rabid and Ripsem!"

With a mournful sigh, Bear clicked off the tv. Recalling another *Simpson's* episode—*The Land of Chocolate*—he supposed he was probably the only fan of the family show still upset by that white chocolate rabbit accusing Homer of wanting to eat

him, then taking off in a failed attempt to outrun...

Arf! Arf! Arf! Arooooo! Arf! Arf!...

"What in blazes are you doing here in the middle of the morning?!" Foxy shouted after barging in. "And... And... are those remains of my hounds' *Stella & Chewy* rabbit patties in your lap?!"

Arf! Arf! Arooooo...

"Hoick! Hoick! Hoick!" the mistress of hounds yelled at him, technically still master of the trailer house for a likely last day.

Arf! Arf! Arooooo! Arf! Arf!...

Out on the stoop with the door slammed shut behind them, Bear informed the wife that he had decided to retire from farming, and...

"Retire?! You've not done a day's work in your life, Bear McGregor! Take that brown thumb outta your ass and git back to your weed patch!"

He was not cut out for a day's . .. for growing weed at a profit, he explained for the hundredth time, and by trying to be a farmer had run up a debt that threatened...

"You have got us in hock to Big Bert Haggard, haven't you. Damnit, 'stead of whining about Killer and paying Big Bert and that buzzard for 'protection', you should have grown a pair of balls and let me get rid of those damn rabbits by staking Killer on a long chain up at that patch of weed."

"I don't give a hoot about that weedy patch anymore, or for the whole dang farm," Bear declared. "I'm goin' to the bank for money to pay off Big Bert, for your sake, Foxy."

"I'll take care of Bert Haggard if he dares to come 'round again and tries to set a spark in the trailer house," said the wife, which was just what Bear was worried about; the wife "taking care" of Big Bert.

"But... But... But what if that cousin comes back around, wantin' to be paid off to go away? I went to town and left her a note, warning her about..."

"Ha! I've already taken care of the 'cousin'. And dang it, for the thousandth time, my Beagles are not dogs. They're fearless

hounds that you should have warned Big Bert about."

Wondering what Foxy had meant by saying that, hoping the wife had "grown a pair" to stop Big Bert from trying to…

"Go on to town and get a bank loan before I sic my hounds on <u>you</u>!"

Bear drooped his head and trudged toward the family pickup truck, muttering to himself that when Big Bert came around tonight to get paid-off—no doubt with intent to "spark" with Foxy—he just might knock the bully's head clean off.

CHAPTER TEN

Max manned the shotgun seat. The kid rode in back. Tots was at the wheel of Mom's brown boiler as they slowly tracked a vaguely familiar rutted dirt road toward the McGregor farm northwest of town. On the radio…

To continue WOKC-FM's observance of the Dog Days of August, here's one by the Twenty Fingers from 1995…

♫Ooh, ah, ooh, ah (Woof! Woof!/ Ooh, ah, ooh, ah, (Woof! Woof!)… ♫

He'd had to lean on Tots to lend a hand, and the Mexican rabbit had finally agreed to come along on condition of being only the "getaway car's" wheel man — "just in case the McGregor cousins' pets are biters"-- even though Yours Truly was packing heat. Yeah, the shoulder-holstered Roscoe — an exact replica of Mike Hammer's "Old Junior" — did not actually squirt lead and his Unarmed P.I. License didn't allow him to carry a lethal weapon, but a dog would likely not be wise to those details.

♫Born with your bow-wow tactics/ Hooked on the C-A-T like addict/ Always thinkin' 'bout your bone/ Tryna take some cutie home… ♫

Max had never had a so-called "man's best friend" or any other kind of pet, not counting his brain that he sometimes thought of as a hamster spinning a wheel inside his head.

In his book, canines posed dangers to humans on a par with secondhand tobacco smoke. In addition to bites, the pesky pets caused countless trips-and-falls. They did their business when and where they pleased, infecting soil with germs lasting for years. Dogs ate low-income families out of house and home. But

oh no, "follow the science" didn't apply to getting rid of "best friends". While a guy would get busted if not stoned for lighting up a stogie on a windy beach…

♫What kitten put you on a leash? Thought she had your ass in reach/ But you can't teach a dog news tricks… ♫

"This is it," said Tots, braking the boiler to a stop at a rusty mailbox. "This is the entrance leading to the farm's, uh, house."

♫Who let them dogs loose?/ (Woof-woof! Woof-woof!)/ Who let them dogs… ♫

With the boiler engine still running and the antsy Hollywood networker in position to put pedal to the metal, Max got out of the getaway car with a brown paper sack in hand.

Ankling down a weedy driveway with the kid at his side, he detected slightly muffled sounds of barking, but… thankfully, no signs of pooping… and, uh, oh, spotting a redheaded dame coming out of a trailer house, he hotfooted to her.

After putting the likely McGregor cousin wise to his name and game, he lifted a leg, so to speak:

"Looking into the disappearance of a Ms. Beatrice McGregor who claimed to be heiress to this acreage."

"Why?" the redhead answered, before copping to being in fact an Evylyn McGregor, no doubt one of the unfriendly cousins who had run his client off the premises. "She waved some paper but wouldn't show the 'will'… "

Dang!

"… and 'disappeared' weeks ago, back into the hole she crawled out of would be my guess."

"Run to ground, huh?" said Max, pivoting slightly from his hunch that the client had tried to pull a scam and, lifting another leg: "Maybe chased by one of the canines you have cooped somewhere around here."

"I 'coop' no 'dogs'," said Evelyn McGregor, obviously lying.

Yeah, Yours Truly's client had crawled back into a hole alright—the local Fountainblue Motel—and got a message, printed in block letters, warning her to 'Bewear uv The Beast".

"Well, don't look at me. I don't write in childish block letters,

and deal only with trained Beagle hounds."

"As in *Hound of the Baskervilles?*" said the kid.

"Who's the overfed pup?" the carrot-top asked.

Max put the now confessed dog owner wise to the also overweight kid being his case report jotter, responsible for jotting notes about everything seen and said during his investigation.

"Dating back to about a month ago, when Ms. Beatrice McGregor's bloody blouse was found in the alley behind the Fountainblue Motel."

"Along with paw prints," the kid added.

"So what? My hounds are kenneled night and day except when hunting rabbits at dusk and dawn under my strict command as their Mistress. No way could or would any one of them wander into town without my instruction."

"Where were you on the night of July 10th, Ms. McGregor?" the kid blurted, with notepad and pencil in hand.

"Here at home," she claimed, with a nod toward the trailer house. "Probably watching *Simpsons* episodes with my mate, Bear. Ask him, if you like. He can usually be found on his weed patch in the north forty, but is not on the farm today."

Pivoting again… "How about this evidence that you yourself might've wandered into town?" said Max, taking the heel-less red shoe from the paper sack.

"Ha! I wouldn't be caught dead in that tarty footwear."

"Who might be 'found' in the south forty?" said the kid, butting in with an irrelevant line of grilling and nod in the direction of an expanse of rocks and ravines.

"No one," the foxy *femme* claimed with an annoyed, if not nervous look in her baby blues. "The south forty is not fit for cultivation, and is even more unfit for habitation by man or beast."

"How 'bout you take off one of your boots and try on the 'tarty footwear'," said Max, tracking the opposite direction taken by Percy Wilson in *Case of Cinderella's Wicked Step-Sister*. In his own case, if the shoe <u>did</u> fit, the dame was illegit. But…

Arf! Arf! Arf!…

"Get off my property before I sic a hound on you!" the suspect screeched. "And don't dare to come back if you value your lives!"

Arf! Arf! Arf! Arooooo...

With the kid trotting beside him, Max hotfooted back down the driveway... hopped into the boiler... and above the radio racket...

♫You ain't nothin' but a hound dog/ You ain't never caught a rabbit/ And you ain't no friend of mine... ♫

... shouted for Tots to put pedal to the metal.

Max's bulldog instinct barked loud and clear: Though maybe not a scamster in cahoots with Tots Lyon, the redheaded canine mistress — obviously crooked as a dog's hind leg — was hiding something.

♫Yeah, they said you was high-classed/ But that was just a lie... ♫

CHAPTER ELEVEN

♫They ran through the briars and they ran through the brambles/ And they ran through the bushes where a rabbit couldn't go/ They ran so fast that the hounds couldn't catch 'em… ♫

Gripping the wheel of the speeding getaway car with knuckles tight and white as a Hollywood starlet's capped teeth, Tots silently cursed his run of bad luck after getting off the bus in the dirtball town of Henryetta, Oklahoma, to take a leak… picking up the unfinished manuscript of the so-called "Maximo Morgan Mystery" from the men's room floor… reading it on his way to visit old high school friends in California… pitching Morgan's *Case of Dogs in a Manger* to the two Stans… and getting involved in the risky business of making a movie.

Any of you cats out in radioland think these Dog Days are bad, don't bite the hand of the WOKC-FM weatherman. According to the Old Farmers Almanac, Greek and Roman wiseguys back in the day doped out that it's Sirius—the freakin' Alpha Canis Majoris a/k/a the Dog Star—that's rising at this time of year and causing the drought, bad luck and unrest that's drivin' man and dog mad. So chill out and howl along with….

♫You can call your dog a mongrel/ You can call your dog a stray/ Just remember in the end/ Every dog will have his day… ♫

Dog-gone-it, *The Woman Who Came to Supper* project might have turned out okay, Tots silently "howled". Based on the lost-and-found footwear evidence in Morgan's case, he had strenuously argued for continued research—not "dogged" investigation—of a *Cinderella* storyline. Stanley Stanley might have gone along with speculation that the missing McGregor

woman had a romantic encounter at the motel, and lost the shoe in flight to the humble family farm where wicked cousins lived.

In the hands of talented writers, and filmed on a Hollywood set — not on-location next door to a farm loomed over by a "Big Mo" — his life might have gone on toward a happy ending in sunny LaLa Land, but…

♫Every dog must know who's master/ Every dog must know who's boss/ But whenever you run faster… ♫

Max Morgan, seated beside him in the boiler, still huffing-and-puffing after escape from "a redhead's hound", was a bulldog alright. And the teenaged kid in the backseat — in addition to also being pear-shaped — was just like his role model. Having "picked up the scent" of an old Sherlock Holmes Adventure — *Hound of the Baskervilles* — that Stanley Stanley would never…

OMG! It dawned on Tots that — worse than Stanley Stanley turning down the movie project — if Stanford Stanley got wind of the grisly *Hound of the Baskervilles* angle, a project might well get the green light and he, the unlucky networker, would be stuck on-location, within striking distance of…

♫Every dog chews his balls/ Every dog can easily scratch/ And when a dog chews his balls/ You know you've met your match ♫

Unlike his creative cousin and partner, Stanford Stanley was strictly a bottom-line mogul, as evidenced by his production of last year's completely tasteless box office hit, *Lassie Comes Home for Yom Kippur*, in which a successor to the famous Collie bitch got beheaded after refusing to atone for serial murder of wildlife. The Stanleys had almost split up over scathing criticism of the S&S Studio by SPCA fanatics, but then jointly accepted an Oscar. So a sequel along the lines of, say, *Son of Lassie Takes Revenge*…

Buzz. Buzz. Buzz…

That would be the Stans now, calling to check and… Oh no, the relentless bulldog picked up the phone from the seat between them and…

"Sorry, fellas, the networker's got his hands full at the moment,

but no sweat. Maximo Morgan is on the lay like a dirty shirt, and you can both take it from Yours Truly…

"Nah, without mitts on a last will and testament, there's no legit inheritance angle along the lines of *Case of the Wabbit Who Came to Supper*, but looks like we might be dealing with a *Case of Hound of the Baskervilles* that…"

Tots took a hand off the boiler's wheel to reach for the phone, but…

"Yeah, bound to be wildlife…

"Nah, Beagles, not Collies…

"Yeah and yeah, but like Chan said in *Case of Easter at Mom's House*, he who hunts two rabbits at same time likely to have no supper…

"Charlie Chan, Chinaman who lent a helpful hand to Frisco flatfoots back in the *Noir*.

"Yeah, Yours Truly will look under every rock and…"

Tots gripped the steering wheel even tighter and pushed his foot even harder. If either Stan found out that a McGregor farm neighbor was a virtual "doppelganger" for the bully they'd known in high school as "Big Mo"…

"Yeah, heh, heh, if there's a will, there's a way, heh, heh, but like I say… Yeah, almost time for chow back here too. I'll keep you fellas in the loop."

Buzzzzzzz…

Entering the outskirts of town, Tots was more than ready to give up the chase for Hollywood fame and fortune… go back to D.C. with his tail between his legs… and in the moldy basement of his modest suburban house, carry on with winemaking, but…

"Remember how Brad Runyon cracked *Case of the Crooked Horse*, Mr. Max?" said the teenaged kid in the backseat. "The original Fat Man searched the victim's hotel room, spotted that wallpaper illustrating a fox hunt had been messed with, and… Maybe Ms. McGregor hid the old man's will in her motel room."

"No such luck in this case, kid. Rooms at the Fountainblue Motel are paneled with knotty pine."

"Yeah, but how about under carpet or…?"

Feeling dragged along by a rabid bulldog on a leash, Tots, as directed, turned the boiler onto Main Street as on the radio...

Listen up to how this dude in the Bible bitched: "My God, my God, why have you forsaken me?... I am a worm, and no man ... For dogs have compressed me; the assembly of the wicked have surrounded me... Deliver my soul from the sword... and from the power of the dog." So to survive these Dog Days we're havin', my advice to you cats in radioland is to put D-O-G up to a mirror, see what it spells backward, and pray for relief.

♫Just me and you and a dog named Boo... ♫

CHAPTER TWELVE

Max again ankled into the Fountainblue Motel's ratty reception area. Again he spotted the bald head of the joint's owner, Hugo Lice, sitting behind the check-in counter, watching tv.

"Gonna have to go over the room occupied by Ms. McGregor a few weeks ago with a comb," he announced, and again got no lip from Lice.

With Tots Lyon and the kid in tow, he crossed an open-air courtyard surrounded by ground-floor guest rooms fronting onto a waterless swimming pool. In a twist to his *Case of a Puzzling Book*—deserving a spot in *Ripley's Believe-It-or-Not*—it turned out that back in the day a local broad had spent steamy nights between the motel's hot sheets with none other than Hugo Lice. 'Course. the motel owner probably had a head of hair back then, but still…

Reminded that implausible love stories were common subplots in even Mike Hammer murder mysteries, Max decided to cut Tots some slack for pushing a romantic angle in the current case, and—as they said about making movies—suspend disbelief that the nervous networker was not on the level.

At a guest room door labeled #13… Hmmm, turned out he didn't need a key, raising the possibility that someone other than Lice and/or motel staff might have beat him to the punch.

Inside the room, however, he detected that its moldy carpet seemed to have not been touched, maybe for years by not even a vacuum sweeper. Nevertheless, he had the kid begin a search for an Old Man McGregor's last will and testament that one of the Hollywood Stans had described on the blower as a "hook"

needed to launch a storyline picking up where *The Wabbit Who Came to Supper* fizzled.

The room was uncomfortably warm, the bed narrow, lumpy and...

"According to Uncle Ralph, a rabbi and a lawyer, the term 'will' means just that: will or desire of a person to control what happens after death," said the always-chatty teenaged jotter from down on his hands and knees. "But there are ancient common laws that limit a dead man's hand. For instance..."

Yeah, now that Max thought about it, probably those cousins would have got a sharp lawyer to prove it was illegit for the old man to bypass his own offspring and give the family farm to an Australian "niece" about as distant as possible, which... now that he thought more about it, shaded if not deep-sixed a motive for the feisty redhead to have sicced a hound on a rival 'heiress".

"Let's blow this flea bag and have a snack," said Max.

His bunkmate, Tots, also in a sweat, got to his feet, but...

"Also according to Uncle Ralph," the gabby kid continued, "you can leave property to anyone you choose, but can't legally control who gets title for generations afterward, and can't legally make unreasonable rules from your grave about what even a next heir can and can't do in connection with ownership of, say, a farm. For instance, Old Man McGregor could not have legally dictated that his niece—or his offspring—got to keep the inherited property only if she or they murrrderred someone. Conversely, a person who kills a property owner or rightful heir can't legally inherit."

Yeah, the bookish kid could be a pain in the *derriere*, Max noted to Tots with a wink.

"And by the way, Mr. Max, I know it's a cliché, but did you happen to have a look under the mattress before parking your backside?"

Max sprang from the room's bed... with the help of Tots, pushed a mattress onto the floor and... Bingo!... picked up a manilla envelope addressed to a Ms. Beatrice McGregor in Sydney, Australia.

With his mitts on the envelope's contents and Tots and the kid looking over his shoulders, he detected handwriting on a yellow legal-size sheet of paper. Sure enough:

Last Will and Testament

I, John Q. McGregor of Okmulgee County, State of Oklahoma, being of sound mind and my ordinary state of health, make this my last will and testament, to-wit:

Whereas I have been sorely disappointed in my son and only offspring, Larry "Bear" McGregor, particularly in his stupidity, laziness, sentimentality, and unwillingness to manage the family farm in a manner that I require; and…

Whereas, I once had high hopes that my daughter-in-law, Evelyn "Foxy" McGregor, was crafty and cold-hearted enough to make up for my son's failings with the help of her hounds, but am now equally disappointed by her lack of bloodthirstiness required for the job…

I therefore give to my niece and sole remaining relative, Beatrice McGregor, all my property and worldly goods, specifically including full right and title to the aforesaid farm. PROVIDED, HOWEVER, THAT SHE SHALL HAVE AND HOLD THE LAND ONLY IF AND FOR SO LONG AS SHE INDUSTRIOUSLY UNDERTAKES BY ALL MEANS TO ERADICATE EVERY SINGLE RABBIT FROM THE PROPERTY!

Lastly, I hereby revoke all former wills by me heretofore made; and in witness that this is my last will and testament, I have written the whole of it in my own hand on one page and have subscribed my name to it by hand on this the 23rd day of June in the year 2025.

John Q. McGregor

"Dang!" Max exclaimed. "This is the exact opposite of *Case of the Wabbit Who Came to Supper*," he detected, which just went to prove Percy Wilson's private dicking rule to be careful not to step in gum with your gumshoes when walking on mean streets populated by scofflaws! But…

"No *problemo*, Max," said Tots. "When we get this project situated inside the S&S Studio 'cutting room', heh, heh, a team of talented 'scrapers'…"

"The will's conditions probably explain why Ms. McGregor

wouldn't show the will to anyone until she got a lawyer," the kid opined. "She probably thought eradication of rabbits would be declared cruel and unusual. "Yes!" Tots exclaimed. "These illegal conditions might as well have been written in erasible ink."

"The heiress probably should not have worried," the kid continued. "Heck, rabbits gnaw farmers' crops and irrigation lines, spread diseases, and their burrowing causes soil erosion that makes land useless. They reproduce like... like rabbits, and only a few equal a cow's consumption of pasture grass. On the other hand, if the will was declared legal, Ms. McGregor might not have wanted to be obligated to..."

"No need to let complicated legal technicalities get in the way of the story," the Hollywood networker advised. "When the disappeared damsel meets and falls in love with, say, an avid rabbit hunter..."

"Hold the phone!" Max shouted. "There's a second sheet of paper stapled to the will, with handwriting on it."

Back to looking over his shoulders...

"Oh no!" Tots exclaimed.

"Oh yes!" the kid exclaimed.

"Hmmm," Max hmmmed as he perused the second yellow page titled *Codicil* and detected... Yeah, like a simmering pot of rabbit stew, the plot in *Case of the Woman Who Came to Supper* thickened.

CHAPTER THIRTEEN

With a brown paper sack in hand, Bear trudged alongside the weedy driveway of the McGregor family farm in descending darkness. Though worried about missing Bert Haggard to settle his debt, he was too tired to trot. He'd been delayed in town, and in the hot August weather the family pickup truck had overheated miles ago. Noticing that no lights were on in the trailer house and no one outside, he collapsed into an unfolded lawn chair set next to the trailer's front-door stoop and gripped the brown paper sack tighter.

According to the man at the bank, the farm was too worthless for a mortgage. And on top of other expenses his income from farming together with what Foxy earned by breeding, training and selling Beagle dogs would not be enough to cover payments on a plain personal loan. But the wife and him had some savings stored there, and after going from place to place to look for a job, he had wandered onto the Dean Motor Company used car lot.

Inside an air-conditioned office, Mr. Dean admitted that he was getting up in years, that his grown son was lazy, that he hisself didn't like pulling his tow truck up too close to houses of deadbeats, and that he could use a hand to help repossess cars that had unpaid debts leaning on them. So after he had proved to Mr. Dean that he could lift up the back-end of vehicles and drag 'em for a city block or more without making a sound, the car lot owner had agreed to not only hire him, but to lend a hand by paying two-week's wages in advance.

Bear sighed. There was still not enough money in the paper sack to pay Big Bert all he was owed for past weed patch

protection from rabbits, but…

Arooooo…

That would be one or another of Foxy's dogs out on the south forty, he reckoned. Since the start of Summer two months ago, the wife had made a habit of taking nighttime walks, usually with the runt named Snoopy that had trouble settling down after early evening hunts. But…

Dang it, Bert Haggard's farm butted up to the south forty. The big bully—thankfully without that eagle-eyed falcon at night—would be coming to the trailer house by that way and might butt up to Foxy, or… Bear couldn't help from thinking the wife might be intending to…

Arooooo…

He had got his nickname because—like the Br'er Bear character in old cartoons—he was easy to trick. Yep, back in high school he was all the time being invited to go on snipe hunts, by hisself. Only lately he had started to wonder if any such varmint such as a "snipe" even lived in these parts. And Foxy had joined in making fun, by inviting him time and again to go—with her—to watch nighttime submarine races out at Possum Pond. Again, he'd never spotted nothing. But holding hands in the front seat of her daddy's station wagon had led to them becoming sweethearts in the back seat.

But that was a long time ago, and since then…

♫ *I'm the fastest bird of prey/ Bird of prey, bird of prey…* ♫

Bear stood up… stuffed the sack of money into his pants… grabbed a big bag of dried rabbit patties off the stoop… and set out for the south forty.

♫ *I find the highest perch to roost/ Perch to roost, perch to roost…* ♫

Dog-gone-it, it had just then sunk into his head that he should have knocked Bert Haggards head clean off yesterday.

Arf! Arf! Arf!…

Arrived at the dog pen, Bear set about emptying the bag of dried rabbit patties, and…

Arf! Arf!…

… when the pack got quiet and started eating… Dang it,

though he couldn't say for sure how many hounds the wife kept—Foxy was all the time telling him her "darlings" were hounds, not dogs—he saw that the runt, Snoopy, was not out walking with the "Mistress".

♪*My talons and beak are fierce/ They can surely, surely pierce/ Surely pierce, surely pierce...* ♫

Bert Haggard wouldn't need a fierce falcon to get what he wanted, Bear fully realized as he picked up a big stick and plunged deeper into the south forty by dim light of a half-moon, made off-and-on dimmer by passing clouds. The neighborhood bully was hisself a fierce bird of prey...

♪*Bird of prey, bird of prey...* ♫

And wouldn't be satisfied until he got hold of Foxy.

♪*Bird of prey, bird of prey...* ♫

Sensing the sumbitch had recently passed nearby, Bear was sorry he had argued the wife into getting rid of the hound named Killer and... Oh no, in a flicker of moonlight... on the rocky ground... blood... and sticking out from a cluster of scrub brush... a stark white lifeless-looking human hand.

CHAPTER FOURTEEN

♫*People may laugh, but I don't mind/ They'll never understand the kind of fun I find...* ♫

With the kid riding shotgun, Tots in the back, and a memorable dance tune echoing inside his bean, Max drove the boiler down a rutted dirt road that even in nighttime *noir* he now recalled traveling, not only earlier in the day on his way to the McGregor farm, but also three years ago in connection with *Case of Deadly Droppings.*

♫*Doin' the pigeon (coo) (coo)/ Doin' the pigeon (coo) (coo)...* ♫

Yeah, this would not be Yours Truly's first tango with a dude named Haggard. In the course of investigating a client's pigeon racing rival — a dame named Coo Coo Haggard — he'd attended a Fine Feathered Friends wingding at the VFW Hall. When the client cut in on Coo Coo and him, he'd found himself coupled cheek-to-cheek for a few pigeon steps with her tall, awkward husband, Bert.

♫*Doin' the pigeon (coo) (coo)/ Doin' the pigeon coo) (coo)...* ♫

And now the tall, clumsy palooka was Suspect *Numero Uno* in *Case of The Woman Who Came to Supper.* Yeah, by dead hand Old Man McGregor had scribbled and stapled a second page- - titled *Codicil* — to his last will and testament that made his "likeminded and trusted neighbor, Gary Lee 'Bert' Haggard," the will's Executor, fully empowered to enforce its terms and conditions. And had further provided that if his niece — Beatrice McGregror — failed to pledge in advance and "thereafter ferociously pursue eradication of rabbits" from the family farm, title to the property would go to Haggard.

Yeah, it was still the exact opposite of the *Wabbit Who Came to Dinner* scenario that the creative Hollywood Stan was on the lookout for. But the kid was happy as a dog with two tails that detection of a neighbor and rival heir fitted into a *noirish* set-up along the lines of Sherlock Holmes' *Case of The Hound of the Baskervilles.* Tots, however, not so much.

At dinner in Mom's kitchen following Yours Truly's detection of the documents stashed or forgotten at the Fountainblue Motel, the Hollywood networker had babbled almost incoherently about running into Bert Haggard at the neighboring Haggard farm yesterday, along with a dangerous "doppelganger" and falconer.

♫*Dancin' a smidgeon of the kind of ballet that sweeps me away...* ♫

Only after Yours Truly had offered to pay for a ticket on tomorrow's eastbound bus did Tots drop his suitcase and give up his plan to hitchhike back to Washington, D.C. Only after the kid had guaranteed that a falcon would not be out at night, were they able to drag the frightened Mexican rabbit into the back seat of the boiler for a drive-by if not a face -to-face with Haggard and possibly the doppelganger named Donald. Probably brothers, possibly twins, Max had doped out; possibly living together on their family farm and possibly in cahoots to eliminate Beatrice McGregor in order to...

"Stop!" Tots shouted, obviously getting colder feet. "Turn around," he cried as the McGregor mailbox appeared in the boiler's headlights. "I saw flickers of flashlights in the field back there."

Max suspected the once hot-to-trot Hollywood networker's feet had frozen. Truth be told, his own toes had gotten a little chilly, but...

"We'd better look into what's going on," said the kid. "Not to worry, Mr. Max, neither would the redheaded cousin have her Beagle hounds out hunting at night. Not with coyotes, even wolves, not to mention bears out and about."

Against his better judgement, but eager to close the case, Max backed up the boiler... got out of the ride... checked that his Roscoe was securely shoulder-holstered... and also with a

flashlight in hand, followed the kid into an unfenced rocky field.

The nighttime foray without well armed National Guard back-up made no sense, he immediately realized. But Mom, in addition to telling all her friends about the movie project, had bought a new dress for a gala Hollywood premiere. The kid had argued that for *Case of The Woman Who Came to Supper* to be made as a murky *noir* film shot on-location, the finale would have to be at night. And Tots, limping along behind them…

Arooooo…

"May Day!" Max hissed. "Back to the getaway car ASAP! Every man for himself!"

Arooooo…

"Probably just a love-sick coyote, and in the distance," said the kid, ploughing ahead and…

Arooooo…

Max detected the unmistakable aroma of rabbits being barbecued on a charcoal grill… saw the glow of a campfire up ahead… and picked up a murmur of… people laughing?

Hmmm.

After stumbling onward… he unholstered his Roscoe and barked: "Nobody make a move!"

"You again!" the redheaded McGregor cousin barked back, rising from a rock with a sharpened stick in hand. "I warned I would sic my hound on you, and Killer is now out and about."

Killer?!

"This is my brag-hound's home, and he does not take kindly to intruders."

"Who's the other woman that's come for a late-night cookout?" said the kid, aiming a flashlight beam in the direction of… a couple huddling like scared rabbits on a large rock, including none other than…

"She's my dear cousin, Beatrice," the redhead admitted, bold as a hooker in church. "Bea and my dear brother, Todd, have been staying in that cave over there under Killer's protection," she said, pointing the stick, "until Todd's, uh hasty departure from the county jail in Okmulgee gets sorted out."

Without Yours Truly needing to do any third-degree grilling, the foxy dame copped to being wise to Old Man McGregor's will, including the second page making Bert Haggard a dangerous rival to her cousin's inheritance… to sending her brother, a Todd Reynard, to the Fountainblue Motel, to warn the heiress of the danger, and… like in a sappy movie, the distant second or third-degree cousins had supposedly fallen in love at first sight.

So when the female lovebird got a childish warning about Bert Haggard — sent by the redhead's "simpleminded" husband without her knowing — Reynard and the two dames had got the bright idea to plant a "red herring" in the motel alley to put cops and Yours Truly off their scent and onto Bert Haggard's odor. Now the cozy couple planned to get married soon as the escaped jailbird settled his tab at the county's Iron Bars Hotel, and…

"A perfect Hollywood ending!" Tots declared. "Boy meets girl, etcetera, etcetera."

"Not that Bert Haggard would have had a legal leg to stand on," the feisty carrot-topped dame continued. "Cousin Beatrice, born and raised in Australia — where rabbits have overrun the whole continent — shares her distant uncle's, uh, sentiments toward the pests, and has bonded with Killer. As for the big bully's criminal threats, I myself…"

Arooooo…

At the sound of plodding footsteps behind him, Max swiveled… a hulking figure lumbered from surrounding *noir*…

"Bear!"

… he dropped the Roscoe and raised his hands in surrender.

"What the hell are you doing out here on the south forty?!" the redhead continued. "Didn't you see my note on the fridge?"

"I was worried about you, Foxy," said the brute. "I was afraid you might… butt into Big Bert when he crossed the south forty on his way to collect the money. I left the trailer house to catch… to catch him in the… the act of butting, and to knock his head clean off, but… But I didn't do it, I swear. It must have been Donald that turned on Bert and… and chewed his hand clean off."

"Yeah, Bear, if the sumbitch is dead, it must have been…"

Aroooo…

"A perfect Hollywood ending," the kid exclaimed, "with a *noirish* semi-*Hound of the Baskervilles* angle!"

"Agreed!" said Tots, with a hearty pat on the teenaged case report jotter's back. "Both Stans will love the blended storylines. And you, young man, have a bright future ahead of you in Hollywood!"

The happy campers—including Totchli Lyon and the kid—went back to laughing, but not Max, not yet. Until Yours Truly tracked down and collared Donald Haggard… obviously a wrong number in cahoots with Bert, but a murrrderrrer who turned against his own brother… there would be no Hollywood ending to *Case of the Woman Who Came to Supper*. Not in Yours Truly's book, not unless the kid sold out for fame and fortune as a would-be Tinseltown fact-fiddler with an artist license, and jotted…

Arooooo…

THE
END